Hoodoo Heaven

Boudin, Bourbon, and Barbecue, Volume 0

Reggi Dupree

Published by Reggi Dupree, 2022.

Chapter 1

I met my first ghost around the time I wobbled my first steps. And whew, the dearly departed haven't given me a moment's peace since. If seeing dead people was my only gift, I would be plenty happy, but nope. I'd hit the messed-up motherlode. Trust me, I could've gladly lived the rest of my days without sensing supernatural creatures and occasionally reading auras. The only thing in my bag of tricks that worked in my favor was that my head was too hard to be influenced by vampires. Which really sucked for my Aunt Rose, who had the joy of raising a stubborn, half-wild with grief, and all-human orphan.

In other words, my family was, and still is, the epitome of complicated. The last place a woman who at best held disdain for all things supernatural should be hanging out was a building older than the United States. So how in the seven hells did I wind up standing in the middle the oldest pub in Dublin, a.k.a. ghoul central? I blamed hormones, an obsession with all things whiskey, and a sinfully sexy tattoo artist.

This time I wasn't talking about myself, but Riley, a man who looked too much like Lenny Kravitz for his own good.

Stepping out with a man like Riley, meant bringing it. And baby, I ain't even going to lie, I was feeling myself tonight. Extra twenty pounds be damned, I looked hot. From my locs to my Doc Marten lace up heels, I felt like a million bucks. Beneath my well-loved bomber jacket, I rocked a sexy vintage 1950's wiggle dress in a red that popped against my sepia toned skin.

The Thirsty Pig was majestic in the way of all old things—especially those that specialized in sin or comfort (my two favorite things). Okay, that wasn't exactly true, but they were absolutely in the top three. The bar was dim enough for ambiance, yet bright enough not to make the small but comfy space feel like a cave. The backlit bar and hanging pendant lights felt like a stage with the barkeeps the stars of the show.

Speaking of stars, Riley, the man at the center of more than a few non-alcohol related bawdy dreams, raised a pint of beer so rich it looked chewable. "To Gwendolyn Carter, a colleague, friend, and the best damn tattoo artist on the other side of the pond."

My own glass of twenty-year-old whiskey paused half-way to my lips, and I gave Mr. Banging Body my version of the death glare. "Excuse me?"

"Stay. Change my mind." He smiled, and dear ancestors, the twinkle in those dark brown eyes said he wanted to see more than my artistic abilities.

"Don't tempt me." I would love to stay and chill, but the whole ghost thing wasn't my biggest problem. Nope, I needed to stay alive the next thirty-six hours, which would break the curse placed on generations of women in my direct maternal line.

No big.

"Why the hell would I do that?" He shrugged those broad shoulders, clinked his glass against mine, then took a hearty gulp.

Were neck obsessions a real thing? I'd have to say yes. Because I rubbed my hand against my thigh to keep from reaching up and wrapping my fingers around the side of Riley's.

Lucky for me and the rest of the female population in The Thirsty Pig, for Riley, the cold spring night was a mere inconvenience. Let's just say a long-sleeved black shirt had never looked better. Tight enough to appreciate his nipple bars, but loose enough to hint at a six pack. Honestly, I was torn between annoyed that he'd covered so much of that brown yummy goodness, and relieved that the only visible tats were the flames licking up his neck.

Yesterday, I said my goodbyes to the rest of his staff. Today, I played tourist, checking out the Trinity Library and the famous Book of Kells. After I did some shopping on Grafton Street, then treated myself to a solo picnic on St. Stephens Green. But tonight, Riley, Bridgette, his business partner who happened to be his ex-wife, and I, were hanging out for our last hurrahs, but as usual Bridgette was late, so it was just Riley and I for now.

"Thanks for coming to Dublin. Getting to finally work with you was as cool as I expected," Riley said.

"Ditto." I tossed back my fifth glass of whiskey, savoring the delicious burn sliding down my spine.

I closed my eyes, sinking into it, hoping for once, I'd drank enough to make the ghosts disappear.

I leaned right, cracked open an eye, then muttered a curse so foul the seafaring apparitions in the back corner, had they heard, would've applauded.

Not only were the pirates there, but two dead, busty, and flirty women had taken up residence at the other end of the bar to get their attention.

"Whoa..." Riley grabbed my bicep. "You okay?"

I nodded, and judging from Riley's raised eyebrow, probably a little too vigorously.

"Let's grab an empty table," he said, motioning to the tall four-top three women just left.

"No, I'm good." I crossed my heart with my index finger. "Promise. Besides, I've spent the last week hunched over back-pieces. I could probably stand for the next month." Okay that was a slight exaggeration, but better than Riley thinking I was hammered. Which sucked, because regardless how much I drank, getting good and truly shit-faced remained beyond reach.

But that didn't mean I'd stop trying.

I traced the curved edge of the bar, motioned to the bartender for another round, then smiled up at Riley. "I'm thinking maybe I lived here in a past life." I wiggled my eyebrows.

"Then do it again. Stay. Work with me... or not. I'd like to get to..." Riley bit down on his lush lower lip.

That magnificent kissable mouth of his all but held me hostage. As we stood there, my body screamed—hell to the yes. Until, of course, my brain got involved and pumped the brakes. Because not only had my last few lovers died, but they'd also done it violently. Not only was that a great way to never get a date again, but the cops gave you a nickname—suspect. But with each of the four deaths, I had an airtight alibi. The nickname did change. But… let's say, Black Widow wasn't much better.

So, sleeping with me had a high probability of Riley ending up good and dead. And since I liked him, celibacy was the only option. Sometimes, ten years without sex may as well be a lifetime.

Which meant I was forced to decline with a sad and most unfortunate truth. "My family isn't getting any younger." Not all my people would live long past the time when my body had returned to dust. The thought of burying people I loved bruised my heart. "Plus, I've been on the road too long. I need to go home."

Home…

A place where Black hair care products were plentiful. The place where I could visit a beauty shop, get my locs re-twisted while listening to gossip and laughing as loud as I wanted. Never would I have believed the place I called Mayberry with melanin and magic could be the balm for my wandering soul.

Home…

The place where some people believed I was a murderer.

For the first time in twenty-five years, I might be ready to risk it all for some boudin and Texas barbecue.

But for that to happen I had to survive the next two days. Which would be easier if I could put a name and face to my enemy. I scoped out the other patrons in the bar. Could it be the young dude with the scraggly beard, or maybe even the woman he was with, who looked like she could break him in half?

One thing I learned long ago was that my enemy didn't want an audience, so I surrounded myself with people. Whether it was for protection or cannon fodder, I chose not to examine my motives too closely.

An uncomfortable weight settled in my hollowed-out chest, a distasteful cocktail of hope, longing, and terror.

"Does that mean you'll finally open your own shop?" Riley asked.

"Nah, I'll just work with the family. Hell, they're almost as good as I am." I didn't bother hiding my grin. Hey, when you're the shit, why be modest?

Riley returned the grin, which turned into a smile. The kind of expression you wouldn't mind seeing on the pillow next to you in the wee hours of the morning. "Are you down for a visitor in...? Where in Texas are you from again?"

"Hoodoo." A lovely but almost forgotten Texas town on the outskirts of Houston.

Little lines formed between his brows. "Like in I'll-put-a-root-on-you Hoodoo?"

I leaned back and pressed a palm against my chest. Well, well, well, Mr. Riley was full of surprises. "What do you know about that?"

"Sweetheart, I'm from Ireland. Magic and whiskey run through my veins."

Interesting. Most humans were so wrapped up in creating and sustaining a life they had neither the time nor the will to expand their minds. "So... you believe there's a world beyond our imaginings?"

Riley scoffed. "How could I not? It's hubris to believe we're the only creatures in the universe."

I licked my bottom lip and considered how to respond without sounding like a basket case? If I asked if he noticed not only the ghosts, but the fae in the room he'd think I'd slipped into a perimenopausal psychosis. "True that," I said, nodding in agreement.

The blast of cool air against my legs drew my eye to the door, and I couldn't help but grin at Bridgette as she pranced across the bar in her chic rockabilly uniform, of high-waisted jeans rolled up at the cuffs, saddle shoes, and a black turtleneck.

I nudged Riley with my shoulder as I nodded toward her. "Look who finally decided to join us."

Bridgette ignored her former husband and wrapped me in her steady arms. After air kisses on both cheeks, she held my arms and pulled back. "You, darling, look scrumptious." She pivoted to Riley, giving him a quick kiss on the lips, then looked back and forth between Riley and me. "You two look like Black tatted Ken and Barbie."

"Well thank you, you don't look so bad yourself." Don't ask me how, but their relationship just worked. Not only was Bridgette beautiful, with her quick smile, dark hair, and pale skin, completed by a spray of freckles across her right cheek. But she was as funny as she was talented.

I'd miss her almost as much as Riley.

"Glad you came. But that whole Barbie thing only works if I get to be Ken." I winked at the bawdy Bridgette and struggled with which of the two I'd like to take to bed more. Yup, I was a proud bisexual. So why choose?

Riley leaned in and whispered, his warm breath a caress against my ear. "Bring the right toys, and you can be my Ken."

A wave of heat that had nothing to do with failing hormones blasted through me.

Woo, he needed to stop saying stuff like that before I started shouting like this was a C.O.G.I.C. Sunday service. I rested both of my hands on his narrow hips, then pressed my forehead against his chest. "I wish..."

Riley whispered, "what are you running from beautiful? Maybe I can help."

My eyelids suddenly felt gummy. I patted his chest to get myself together before memorizing Riley's chiseled face and kind eyes. "Somedays, I think it's myself. But that's a conversation for another time." The gaiety in my voice didn't fool either of us judging by his pursed lips, but I smiled anyway. "Tonight, is a celebration."

"Pardon," said a deep voice with an accent tinted by either Oxford University or British colonialism.

Holy crap.

If I typed tall, dark, and deadly in any search engine, this dude's picture would pop up. His ancestry could be from anywhere from Turkey to North Africa, I couldn't tell. What I did know was that his family tree had some beautiful branches, and he'd hit each one on his way down.

The swirling mass of colors surrounding him shifted from amber to violet to black as the void, then back again. It was as if someone shoved eight feet of power and personality into six feet of human male.

The jeans and dark gray cashmere hoodie were expensive, but off the rack. Those shoes, however, would never convince anyone he was an overpaid office worker.

Riley's pec tightened beneath my palm. Who was that man? In the years that I'd known Riley, I'd never seen him shaken.

I sucked in a deep breath.

I've seen hot. Hell, I've inked the most prominent men on the planet: rock stars, rappers, politicians, drug lords, and priests. You name it, I've tattooed them. But nary a one of them came close to this man's swagger—not even Riley.

The power radiating from this intruder was beyond human. Hell, until today, my uncle Raul, one of the oldest vampires in North America was the most formidable man I'd ever encountered.

Until tonight.

A cold bead of sweat rolled down the center or my back. *Ancestors, what was happening?*

For once, an answer, a sign, hell, even a swarm of locust would be nice.

What was that saying about a wish in one hand and shit in the other? Well, I was standing there with a hot stinking pile of one of them, and it didn't feel like a gift from a Jinn.

Was I being paranoid?

Yes, judging by the two male fae rocking biker glamour and their lascivious grins. Then again, they'd seemed bespelled by the cleavage exploding from the bustier of the woman chatting them up. Perhaps they weren't as enthralled as I'd believed. The darker of the two must have felt the weight of my attention, because he turned to me with a wink, and an I-know-you-know-what-I-am look, then placed his index finger against his lips in the universal shh sign, before returning his attention to the boobalicious woman.

I continued to face the bar, keeping my back to Riley and Bridget, but the full focus of my attention returned to this surprise visitor. I didn't believe in much, but I trusted my gut, and it told me that something wasn't right about Mr. Tall Dark and Deadly. What I didn't want was his psychic juju all over mine. But I had no choice.

Someone wanted me dead in the next thirty-six hours, and just my luck, Mr. Testosterone overload would be a carrier for Death Express, the courier service for killers who absolutely, positively, needed their victim delivered on time.

I opened that inner door that the most precious of my powers hid behind. The gift of... I had no true name for it other than cognition. With most beings it was obvious, at least to me, when they weren't human. Especially those who'd never been. Since most people walked through life believing themselves the top of the food chain, there was no need for the supernatural to resort to playing human.

Because, come on, would a lion hide from a lamb?

A power that sure as hell wasn't mine, zipped through my veins, pooling in the fingertips of my left hand as if looking for an escape. Instead of glancing at the hand resting on the bar to make sure it wasn't doing a firefly imitation, (which would be freaky as hell, because hello...human here), I used my small gift to allow Mr. Tall Dark and Deadly's life force to brush against mine.

I sucked in a breath as shaky as my nerves.

Dear Ancestors, the man was...

Human?

I spun around and stared. That couldn't be right.

He extended a hand. "Ash Modeus."

"Whoa." Riley shook off the hero worship long enough to return the greeting. "Of course, I know who you are, but it's nice to finally meet you in person Mr. Modeus."

"Ash is fine. I've long been an admirer of your work," he said giving Riley the tiniest of nods.

I knew evil, and Ash Modeus was a bad man. Was he attractive? Oh yeah, but that didn't mean I was ready to kick my common sense to the curb.

As if my hormones decided to provide a rebuttal, giant wave of lust rushed through me like a hot flash on steroids. I placed my hand on my baby Buddha belly and could damned near feel my ovaries, which had maybe seven eggs left between them, rev up like a coal burning fireplace.

Good thing my brain was in charge tonight.

Riley stood a little taller, hooked his thumbs in his belt loops, and nodded. "Thanks."

Who was this guy? The grand poohbah of Ireland?

Mr. Ash Modeus turned his head, aiming all that attention at me. "Ms. Carter, you're a difficult woman to find."

That heat from a few seconds ago morphed into icy dread.

Not good. Mr. Rico Suave was lethal. Not in a rip-your-head-off-and-go-bowling-with-it kind of way. No, he'd chop it off with a battle axe, then drink a glass of burgundy crushed beneath the feet of French angels.

The word vomit escaped before my brain grabbed hold of the reins. "You should've taken that as a hint rather than a quest."

Bridgette blanched.

Riley placed his hand over mine, squeezing it. Whether as warning or support, I wasn't sure, but I'd bet it was a shut the eff up signal.

"Ah, but what is life without challenges? I find that's what I live for these days." The scary Mr. Modeus shrugged.

"Be careful, that could be bad for your health." I balled my hands into fists and gave him my best I'm-not-impressed face.

The smile that curved his full lips was less ha-ha-you're-a-hoot, and more that the prey had become... interesting.

Judging from the choking sounds coming from Riley's vicinity, I'd made another faux pas. "I take it you're some kind of big deal?" I asked.

"Apparently not enough." Mr. Modeus' voice reminded me of the whiskey I'd drank earlier, smokey, smooth, and strong.

"Was there something you needed?" *See, I could be nice.*

Ash looked from me to Riley, then to Bridgette. The two of them could at least pretend not to be all up in our conversation. Then again, witnesses could be a plus.

"If I could have a moment of your time." Ash left the *in private* part unsaid, motioning to a newly emptied spot at the bar.

What I wanted to do was scream: hell to the no, shank him, and flee the country. Two problems. First, what self-respecting Texan would stab a man? Really? We had way more class than that. We'd be more likely to pull an AR-15 from our back pocket. Secondly, running in heels sucked. So, I chose the option behind door number three. I'd be a grown-ass woman and tell Mr. Fancy Pants to buzz off in private.

I slid my hand from beneath Riley's and nodded. "Be right back."

Mr. Modeus looked from me to Riley and back and grinned. That, more than his power, his perceived money and influence, and even his aura terrified me. Cold dank sweat swam between my breasts. If I didn't believe Mr. Modeus would chase me down with the determination of a cheetah on the plains of the Serengeti, I'd hightail it out of the Thirsty Pig.

So much for me being fierce.

Ash looked back to Riley and said, "I'll return her unaccosted."

I rolled my eyes, snorted, and walked toward a space devoid of both ghosts and testosterone.

"Unless you request otherwise." The warmth of Ash's breath danced along the back of my neck.

I pulled my lips between my teeth, biting back a shiver. "I won't." I spun around, then gasped.

Ash's eyes were so dark there was little delineation between his iris and pupil, reminding me of a moonless night sky. The only thing missing was an occasional comet. Which, even as the thought crept through my mind felt ominous and odd. A shiver marched down my spine before settling into a low-level buzz. I may occasionally want the wrong partner or even cry out for that last piece of chocolate cake, but when it came to danger, my body never lied. And it was telling me to run.

But why?

"Ancestors, a little help would be nice here," I silently prayed.

Mr. Ash Modeus studied me as if reading my every secret, studying my every flaw—and finding me lacking.

The jukebox clicked then buzzed. A familiar congo refrain started and the corner of Ash's lip twitched as the first verse of the Rolling Stones' Sympathy with the Devil began.

My breaths came short, hard, and fast. If I didn't watch it, I'd slip into a full-on panic attack. Get it together woman—he's just a man.

I'd asked for a sign from the ancestors, and woo boy, I sure hoped that wasn't it. I didn't care if dude was Lucifer himself, I wouldn't be asking Ash for anything.

When his gaze returned to mine, I almost wished it hadn't. "You're most... unusual." His voice was almost a purr, reinforcing the comparison to a deadly feline.

Wow. If he was about to give me the—you're not like most Black people speech after knowing me all of three minutes, I might go full-on banshee. What the hell did people think we were, the Borg?

He crossed his arms then drummed his fingers against his chin. "Beautiful and unapologetically outspoken I expected, but the sense of humor caught me off-guard."

Alrighty, that let the wind out of the sails of the U.S.S. Attitude. And honestly, I hated mentally going there, but I was tired, scared, and a little hangry. The world would just have to forgive me for being a shrew inside my head. "So, what can I do you for?" I managed to ask without snapping.

"I'm in the market for a piece, and I want it from you."

I coughed, thumped my fist against my chest, then managed to clear my throat. "Excuse me?"

"A tattoo." He blinked innocently. Then, the man who radiated lust and menace actually smiled.

Woo Lord. If I thought he was dangerous before, the deep dimples and the humor in those inky eyes turned him into something akin to a fallen angel.

In my mind, I was cool, calm, and catty. In reality, the words came out in a prepubescent squeak, "Of course." *Get a grip woman.* "Unfortunately, I'm leaving tomorrow," I said. "But, as you know, Riley does excellent work."

It could have been five seconds or five minutes, but Ash stared. Was this man expecting me to break under the strain of his commanding glare?

Boy, please. Mr. Modeus was locking eyes with a woman who spent her hormonal teenaged years raised by vampires. You don't know side-eye and attitude until you have an auntie who's a member of the undead.

So, there we stood, watching each other, the cacophony of the departed dulling to the faintest of whispers, and the hum of the living disappearing all together until Ash and I stood in our own silent bubble of attitude and will.

Finally, Ash shook his head, the smallest of movements. "He's not you."

"Riley, however, is available. I. Mr. Modeus. Am not."

"Ash, just Ash." His gaze shot over to the bar, and not a single line appeared between his thick dark brows. "Is Riley your lover?"

I jerked back and raised a finger. Whatever the heck hackles were, mine were way up. "Whoa, boundaries dude."

It was time to get away from this overbearing man. Too bad my feet went on strike. They, along with other parts of my body south of the border, seemed to be on team do-the-bad-guy.

Ash continued speaking as if he hadn't been way the hell out of line. "I saw the piece you did on Rufus. He's a friend of yours, no?"

I nodded. Rufus was in my circle of misfits I called friends back in college. Like me and the bestie Kyle, Rufus refused to be shoved in a box. He was a Black, tattooed, country singer, and one of the sweetest people I'd ever met.

And our friendship wasn't public knowledge. So perhaps Mr. Modeus wasn't an organ snatching gun runner.

Mr. Modeus was persistent if nothing else, so he kept talking. "I've chased you through two continents."

"There are laws against that, Mr. Modeus."

"Ash," he snapped.

I smiled.

Good. No reason I should be the only person off-balance. And why did he have to smell so yummy? Resisting his devilish ass would be easier if he smelled like fire and brimstone rather than the subtle cologne that suggested sex and satin sheets.

"Laws are for sheep. You and I are creatures who create our own rules. Live our own reality." He shrugged, managing to appear simultaneously innocent and menacing.

I had the urge to baa like one of Bo Peep's finest, but I refrained—barely.

"Should your circumstances change—" A matte black business card with raised gold lettering appeared between his index and middle finger.

"They won't." I raised my chin and balled my hands into fists to keep them from shaking, or punching him, or running my hands down his arms to see if they were as hard as I'd imagined. I glanced over at the bar and Riley; his face clouded with concern.

Bless his heart.

I winked. Then, as the deep lines around Riley's mouth eased, my body grew soft.

After a certain age, no matter how well-maintained, women graduated from hot chick phase. That's cool. Hell, that was life and evolution and all that hoo-ha.

But regardless, I appreciated how Riley looked at me, made me feel. Because the truth of the matter was that I could tell myself I was a bad bitch every morning and night—but it meant more coming from someone else.

"Miss Carter." Ash snapped not only his voice, but his fingers. "Would a hundred thousand dollars change your mind?"

I almost gave myself whiplash. Well damn. Riley wasn't the only thing good for the ego. But hello, someone was trying to kill me. It may not be Mr. Just Ash, but he could be the U.P.S. for kidnappers. Seriously, he wouldn't even need weapons. Dude was a sexy Pied Piper. And I had no intention of following this one anywhere.

"I have a prior commitment."

"Reschedule it," he said, the words sounding more like an order than a request.

"Which part of no did you not understand?" I drew on my breathing exercises, inhaling slowly before things got ugly. Whew, I did not want to show my entire behind in this bar, but this man was pushing his damn luck.

"Should your situation change." He slid the card into my jacket pocket without removing his gaze from mine.

"I won't."

"In that case." He executed a half bow that would have impressed the most hardened courtier. "It was a pleasure," he said, his voice holding laughter and something that sounded like a hint of promise. Ash retreated a step, nodded to Riley, then walked through the door and into the foggy night.

Dramatic much?

"What did he want?" Riley stood beside me, watching the door as if he expected Ash to steal me away, leaving a changeling in my wake.

"Something I don't have—time." I shivered.

Riley wrapped a strong arm around me, making me feel almost safe.

What a joke. Safety was a fairytale when you lived in a world where nightmares walked the streets. There was no Prince Charming for me. Nah, it would be the big bad wolf, someone who'd fight dirty and survive.

Riley cupped my cheeks with his work roughened hands and studied my face. I could get used to this, being treated like the most precious of porcelain, valued for all my jagged little pieces.

I was tired.

Tired of running, tired of waiting, tired of expecting the piano to drop on my head. I clenched my teeth because what I wasn't too tired to do was surrender.

"Are you sure you're okay?" he asked.

I nodded, then sighed. "I am now." I forced joviality into my voice, and raised my chin, ignoring the two nearby ghosts who looked like they should be singing sea shanties.

Crossroads held power. In retrospect, I wished I'd realized that a few moments in a Dublin pub would change the path of my life so drastically.

Chapter 2

After standing in a bar a few hours, it was nice to be outside in the fresh but chilly night air. Riley and I left Bridgette with a couple of her friends and decided to hoof it to my B&B.

Dublin really was a cool city. Yes, crime existed in urban areas everywhere, but it saddened me how much safer it felt to be a woman walking at night in countries other than my own. And we won't even talk about the police.

As much as I looked forward to seeing family, and finally settling down in one place, reentry to the good old U.S. of A added a layer of anxiety I felt nowhere else.

Riley and I paused at the curb. "Are you planning to call Ash?" Riley asked, thankfully interrupting my pitiful thoughts.

"I'm surprised it took you so long to ask." I stepped onto the uneven cobbled street, ignoring Riley's snort.

"That wasn't an answer." He gently poked my arm with his elbow.

While we waited for the light to change, I studied every stranger, inspected every shadow, and remembered the immediate goal—stay alive.

The little walking man on the street crossing sign lit up, a beam of white mixed in beneath the yellow tinted streetlights, and the slow chirp for visually impaired people began.

I stopped in the middle of the road, ignoring the quickening chirp and the waiting cars. "Then how's this: no. I want nothing to do with Mr. Ash Modeus. If I never see him again, my life would be all the better."

Riley tilted his head to the side and frowned, reminding me of a chocolate lab with an afro. "That's... extreme."

A forest green Mini Cooper honked.

"Come on woman." Riley grabbed my hand and tugged me to the sidewalk, laughing. "You're not right in the head."

"You say that as if you hadn't figured it out already." I laughed, and it felt so good. And for the briefest of moments, I was happy.

"Here's the deal, the man is legit. Let's just say inking him could change your life in ways you can't imagine."

I didn't have my own reality show, but I did alright. Between guest appearances on friends' projects as a judge or mentor, my art, and textiles, I didn't need life changing money. I had plenty. "I like my life just fine." I shook my head. "Look, my instincts are rarely wrong. And they're telling me to stay away from Mr. Modeus."

"What are they saying about me?" he asked, lust and his beautiful Irish lilt thickening his voice as he interlaced his fingers with mine.

"That you deserve someone with less baggage."

"You've met my ex; I seem to have a type."

"How about this?" I tilted my head. "I'll be unloading some of that baggage soon. If you're still interested, then..." I shrugged.

Riley pivoted, moving in front of me, cupping the side of my neck. "I will be."

I sighed. "Dude, why do you have to be so nice?"

"One of us has to be." His droll voice was tinted with laughter.

"Ouch." Heat washed from my neck to my ears. Thank goodness for the darkness, maybe Riley wouldn't notice the embarrassment painting my face burgundy.

He winked, then we resumed our journey down the dark sidewalk.

As Riley chatted about an upcoming convention in Amsterdam and the art show he was putting on in a small local gallery, I made noises and nodded in what I hoped were appropriate places as I scanned the street.

Evil stalked us through the night. I sensed it but couldn't pinpoint the source. The fog thickened, rising like steam, covering the buildings with a dull white coat of gloom, then spreading across the sidewalk, parting for us like a wayward flock of sheep.

Scratching, like sharp razor-like claws against the concrete grew closer. The combination of the opaque fog and the darkness left me disoriented as the sound echoed in the macabre and shifting night.

My heart tried to punch through my chest. I tucked my body against Riley's, to remind myself that this wasn't a nightmare. Was I strong? Yes. Would I fight? Absolutely. But damn, I was tired of doing it alone. Even superheroes had a squad—where was mine?

Out of danger, hopefully.

The rasping sound grew closer. What was that movie about the outsider who controlled a mob of marauding rats? Nope, not going there. Especially since those rats killed and ate people.

"Whoa, look at that." Riley pointed to a whirlwind of half-dead leaves dancing closer.

My scalp prickled. I jerked my chin toward the street while keeping my eye on the approaching anomaly as more debris joined the dance. "Let's cross here."

His large hand at the small of my back, Riley guided me to the curb. We paused, as an old-school yellow cab sped by. I specifically chose a place to stay that wasn't in the Temple Bar neighborhood so I could have a bit of quiet. But this was too much like a tomb.

"Are you okay?" he asked. "You seem a little skittish."

All I could do was paste on a smile. Now, if we were dealing with hooligans, or a runaway car, I'm certain Riley would step up and throw down. But I suspected this wasn't that kind of fight.

So, I did what any woman in my position would—I lied. "You know how it is, going over my packing checklist."

My damsel in distress moment had passed, and it was nice while it lasted. I released Riley's arm and slid the two chopsticks from my hair. The one silver, the other iron, and both sharp enough to slice through skin.

Some creatures, like the fae were injured by iron or lead. Others, like shifters, silver was their kryptonite. But two things would end a fight with just about anything—chopping their heads off or a stake through an eye or an evil heart. Since carrying around a battle axe was out of the picture, I'd have to get stabby.

"Speaking of packing—"

I shook my head. "I already have a ride but thank you." We paused at the alley, and the stairs leading up to the entrance to my room. Riley wasn't basketball player tall, but I was five-seven, and even wearing heels he towered over me. But I enjoyed feeling dainty—at least with him. Because with Riley, small, female, and human didn't equate weak. "I had an incredible time. It was just what I needed."

His expression was somewhere between flattered and smug, and completely adorable, if you could use that word for a fifty-year-old man. "I wasn't kidding when I said I would like to come visit you in bum-fuck, Texas."

"Hey now, be nice." I chuckled, wrapping my arms around his shoulders. "I'd like that."

A sleek black BMW crept down the street, its engine growling like a hungry beast begging to be set free.

"You should get inside." Riley's fingers tensed against my hips.

I leaned my head against Riley's and tightened my hold as I stared at the dark area across the street. In that patch of bottomless night, something glowed red. Two somethings—that looked like eyes.

Then, a searing pain zipped up my arm, something akin to the time I stepped barefoot on the home of a zillion fire ants. I balled my fists and struggled to control the shiver of trepidation.

Riley released me, pulled back, then placed a finger beneath my chin, and a soft kiss against my lips. "I'll stay here until you lock the door."

"Hey, maybe you should get a taxi or something." Who or whatever was on the other side of that crimson gaze might need a snack, and I didn't want it to be Riley. As much as I'd like to believe it a coincidence that something powerful enough for me not to sense happened to chill in the shadows near my bed and breakfast, even I wasn't that dense.

"No worries, it's a great night for a walk." Both his voice and his expression held humor.

It was easy to forget that in some places people walked the streets without worry and without weapons.

Finally, I nodded. "Okay. And you'd better not be kidding about the visit."

"Never." He gave me a quick hard kiss then spun me around. "Now go."

I wanted to take the steps two at a time, but just my luck I'd fall on my face trying to be cute. When I reached the door—without falling, thank you very much—the strategically placed pieces of tape I had placed before I left were undisturbed.

While the relief was temporary, I enjoyed it all the same. I smiled down the narrow stairs appreciating one last look at Riley's angular face. "Hey, when you come to Texas, don't be such a gentleman."

He barked out a laugh, winked, then disappeared into the night.

I specifically chose this B&B and this room because the house sat next to an alley and mine was the only room with a secondary exit. It was bad enough I was in a house full of people, placing them in potential danger, which was selfish as all get out. But my pursuer didn't like an audience. That took the whole safety in numbers bit to a whole new level.

Did I want other people to die? Of course not. Did I see their lives as expendable? No. But was I willing to risk strangers rather than my family? Ab-so-fucking-lutely.

I dashed into the room, slammed and locked the door, then pressed my back against it. With my subpar human eyes, I glanced around expecting an early birthday present—like a garrote wielding assassin.

Nothing.

"This is good, right?"

Even the small round night table I'd placed against the door leading to the main hallway sat undisturbed.

"Okay, think, think, think," I mumbled as I rubbed my fingernails against each other.

The other guests at the bed and breakfast were old. Like one foot in the grave and the other on a banana peel kind of elderly. No way in hell could I let that...whatever they were come inside after me. They'd give all of us a shove into the afterlife.

But running screaming into the night didn't seem like the brightest of ideas either.

I was torn between hoping the red eyes belonged to a random hungry predator and took off after Riley, which meant I was not his target, or that he'd left Riley alone and alive. The poor man didn't deserve to die just for being gentlemanly enough to see me home.

Caca.

I threw my jacket on the bed then changed with a quickness that would make a stripper proud. It was time for fighting and fleeing clothes: a sweater, jeans, and cowboy boots.

That took all of five minutes. Now what?

I plopped down on the bed and leaned forward, placing my head between my knees, breathing like I'd run a fifty-meter dash. And as out of shape as I was that meant I may as well be having an asthma attack.

This waiting was torture, and I wasn't into that kind of pain. Now if we were talking about pulling my locs and spanking my ass until I called you zaddy—then we could talk.

"You can do this." I nodded and stood, repeating the world's worst pep talk, as I crossed the dark room to one of the lace-covered windows. After a not-even-close-to-fortifying breath I barely tugged aside the drapes.

Those red eyes had left the shadows.

Just my luck they were not attached to a rabid kangaroo or even a giant freaking rat. No, that would be too simple. They belonged to a man dressed like he'd stepped straight out of a Humphrey Bogart movie.

"Seriously?"

He grinned, exposing a ginormous set of canines.

The fanged face prick created a gun with his empty hand, miming pulling the trigger. Then he decided to really show his behind. He flicked his fingers at the streetlamps. With each gesture the glass globes shattered, falling like brittle raindrops against the sidewalk. He crossed the deserted street, standing beneath the last beam of light and motioned for me to join him as if inviting me to high tea.

Yeah right. I flipped him off, and the last of the streetlights exploded—without the dramatic gesture. I was in so much trouble—and not the good kind.

Mr. Fang Face's high-pitched laughter battered my shields before he said aloud, his voice echoing through the night, "Do it little mouse. Run."

Oh no he didn't. I exhaled fear then inhaled the strength and fortitude given to me by the ancestors.

I stretched my neck from side to side. It may be futile, but if this was the night I died, I would resist to the very end. Using the words of the great philosopher and philanthropist Samuel L. Jackson, I mouthed, 'not today, motherfucker.'

Chapter 3

Like a giant dork, I stood in the middle of the room wearing my backpack and cradling my work toolkit against my chest.

This wasn't the ideal time for my lungs to go on strike. But I allowed myself exactly ten point five seconds to freak out and another two seconds to relearn how to breathe.

"Think, think." I stretched my neck from side to side and rolled my shoulders. If I were an evil bastard planning to murder a wonderful middle-aged woman, I'd place people in the back alley and flush out the target.

So, I could either dash out the side or front doors into certain death or chose the back exit and likely death.

Like Thelma from Scooby Doo, I crept to the door leading to the main hallway, pressing my ear against the wood.

Silence.

"Alex, I'll take likely death for a thousand, please," I whispered and grabbed the doorknob. Just as the door opened, I recalled my visit to The Cathedral of the Holy Trinity. Organized religion and I may have a complicated history, but some battles aren't solo ventures. On my visit to the beautiful church, I got prayed up, accidentally on purpose stole a handful of communion wafers, then filled an empty water bottle with holy water.

Stealing was wrong, but so was getting murdered. I figured the Lord wouldn't mind helping a sister out.

After tossing my backpack on the floor I dug out my measly weapons. Then I chucked wafers at the other door, strategically placed two on each windowsill, including the small rectangular window in the shower, then shoved the bright orange water gun filled with holy water in my jacket pocket. When I slipped into the hall, I was armed with more than chopsticks and an attitude.

Except for the muffled snores of Ms. Bannon and my palpitating heart, the B&B was silent.

Did abject terror burn calories?

Maybe, but not a diet plan I'd recommend.

I crept down the hall, then down the twisty back staircase, ensuring my feet stayed on the carpeted runner. Looked like all those years of playing the floor is lava paid off.

Finally, I stood in the center of the cavernous kitchen waiting for my eyes to adjust.

Now what? I slipped my hand in my pocket, rubbing my thumb across the water gun. If anything other than a vampire was out there, I may as well toss handfuls of marshmallows.

This kitchen was a cook's dream, well at least my idea of a perfect workspace. It was large, open, and homey. But the appliances would fool you if you didn't look closely. The stove appeared antique, but the double ovens, eight burners, and griddle were top of the line. And the subway tile...

I grinned.

There, shimmering in the faint moonlight, hanging from a magnetic strip were a line of stainless-steel knives. Wooden stakes would've been better, but most folks didn't have those hanging around.

Plus, the whole begging and choosing thing.

First, I selected a long thin knife, slipping it between my sock and the sturdy leather of my boot. Then carefully, I pointed and flexed my foot a few times. It would suck if I sliced my ankle open trying to be Jane Bond.

So far so good.

I stared at the line of knives, then added the butcher knife and a cleaver to my paltry arsenal.

"Where's a flame thrower when you need one? Heck, I'd even take a .380." I snorted, as if anyone outside the state of Texas hid firearms in the cookie jar. Right about now, I regretted not carrying more than razor sharp stakes and holy items. Concealed knives were illegal in Ireland, but I'd have to take my chances with the Garda. When it came down to it, I preferred becoming a resident of the Dublin jail than moving into a crypt.

I skulked to the back door, peeked through the curtains, and damned near shat my pants.

Across the alley, one of the biggest males I'd ever seen in my life leaned against the wall. Not only did he look like he used trees for toothpicks, but he hadn't even bothered to play human. Okay, that was a bit dramatic, but dude had to be over seven feet tall.

His eyes narrowed before he grinned. Uncrossing his massive arms, he crooked a finger in invitation.

What was with these jerks?

I sank to the floor, wrapping my arms around my bent knees. I was going to die tonight, wasn't I? That really sucked.

I dropped my shield a little to see what other monsters were in the neighborhood. Hey, the more the merrier. Like I used to do as a kid, I rocked back and forth. I didn't want to go out like this. Not now, not when I was inches from freedom. Many women lamented turning forty-five, saw it as the beginning of the end. Not me. I wanted to live. I wanted to not pay for the sins of a woman long dead. But more than any of that I wanted a way to get out of this house without anyone—especially me—getting dead.

I straightened my legs and tapped the back of my head against the door, hoping to shake loose a miracle, or at least a half-way tenable idea. After a few seconds and the beginnings of a good-sized goose egg, I came up with...absolutely nada.

"Okay ancestors help me out. How about this? If you get me out of this situation, I'll uh... How about I set up an altar and do you guys right? Not only will I return to Hoodoo, but I'll also return to you. Deal?"

Hell, I'd give up a lesser used body part, to make it to sunrise.

I waited for an answer or a burning bush. Hey, I hadn't had sex in ten years. I was almost a virgin again, maybe an angel would come. I waited a few more seconds.

No angel.

No rescue.

No answer.

Oh well, what was I expecting? Divine intervention?

"Yeah right." I grabbed my tool kit and stood. I had a knife in one hand and a case in the other.

A small chirp came from the ceiling, and I damned near leapt out of my skin. Maybe that was the bat signal to run. I glanced from the back door to the front of the house.

Vamp or hot Sasquatch? Not the best of options, but unless I planned to take these old folks to the other side, I had to choose.

The chirp happened again, but this time, I glared around the room, wishing lasers would shoot out of my eyes. The sound quickened, and I searched for the source. The smoke alarm needed freaking batteries. The high-pitched noise set my teeth on edge. I should rip the thing from the ceiling.

Wait—the smoke alarm!

I ran over to the counter, dropping my backpack on the floor before putting my tool kit and pilfered knife on the counter. Then I dragged the tall ladderback stool from the side counter, placing it beneath the flashing red light. Maybe I did have help from the other side. Right there, on the counter sat the crumpled pages of the Irish Times.

"You don't have to tell me twice," I whispered as I dug through the drawers like a cavewoman on her quest for fire.

After snagging a box of wooden matches I kissed them and whispered, "Thank you." Perhaps the universe had been talking; but I've been too busy running to listen.

No more.

I scurried up on the chair and got to work. The long wooden matches were something I'd not seen in ages. I struck one against the side of the box, sighing in relief at the dancing blue and orange flame.

A noise from the front of the house made my lungs, my arm, and my heart stop working. What was that? Another sound, this one dreaded and familiar sent the once frozen lungs into overdrive. The bell like tinkle of breaking glass made me flinch and damned near set my hair on fire.

I tucked the rolled-up newspaper under my arm, then double checked my pocket for my water gun. Still there.

Soft footfalls climbed the front staircase. The vampire could have entered silently but chose not to. Terror was his game, and he played it well.

Time was up.

No more thinking, no more praying. If this didn't work, it was over. And bubba, that didn't work for me. I lit the rolled sports section smiling as the smoke thickened and spread before wafting higher, coaxing the smoke alarm to life. Then like audible dominoes the rest of the alarms in the former mansion blared.

I hopped off the stool, tossed the flaming paper in the sink, then dumped rest of the Times on top.

A hysterical giggle bubbled up in my chest, as I grabbed the old-school black telephone, complete with stretchy cord, then dialed 112, the emergency number posted on the wall. "There's a fire at 47 Shannon Way. Hurry."

After putting my backpack on and grabbing my kit, I was tempted to check to see if hot Sasquatch was still out back, but people were shuffling to the first floor. So, I slipped out the kitchen and joined the rumpled and sleepy crowd.

Then, like the captain of her scone-filled ship, Mrs. McKinnon shooed her guests out the double doors to the dark sidewalk. "Gwendolyn, go on outside."

"Yes ma'am. I hope everything is okay."

"Don't worry yourself!" she yelled over the screeching alarms.

I grabbed, Mrs. Bannon's trembling arm and helped her to the door. "It's okay, I got you. You'll be back upstairs snoring in not time."

"From your lips to God's ear," she said as we shuffled forward.

Guilt was a useless emotion, but I was filled with it. Not for being a bitch, putting random people at risk, but placing these particular sweet old people in the line of fire.

Risking one last look up the stairs, I spotted the vampire. He glared at me, as his power slammed against my shields. Fang-face's eyebrows shot up to his hairline, and his gaze held mine. Rare was the human capable of withstanding a vampire's compulsion. I was one of the lucky ones. But I wasn't stupid. Just because they couldn't break my mind didn't mean my body would fare as well.

I ripped my gaze away, then adjusted my grip from Miss Bannon's jiggly arm to her elbow. "Watch your step." I guided her down to the sidewalk, then jogged up the stairs while slipping one of my silver stakes out of my pocket.

That whole having to be invited inside didn't matter in hotels and public establishments. But that didn't mean he wouldn't break the most sacred of rules, not only for vampires, but all supernaturals. Secrecy was everything. Slaughtering half a dozen elderly tourists would bring unwanted attention.

If that jackass thought I would just stand by and allow him to harm any one of these people, it wasn't going to happen. Not on my watch.

I jogged around Mrs. McKinnon and a clueless pajama clad man carrying a massive suitcase, slid across the tiled vestibule, and flung the silver stake at the vampire's chest.

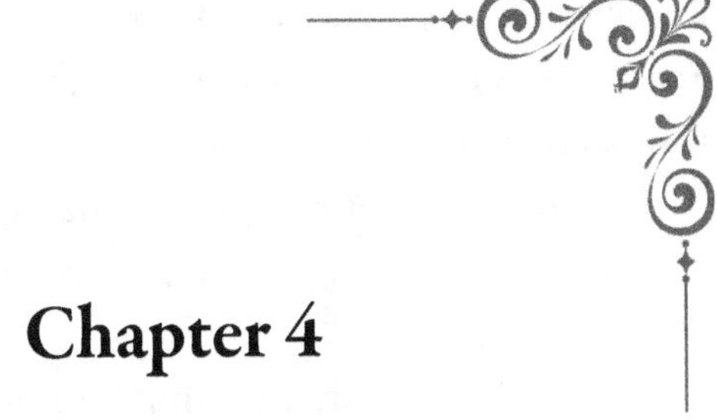

Chapter 4

Overnighting in train stations and airports sucked, even in the best circumstances. But huddling on the floor between two whirring and coughing vending machines, and within sniffing distance of the bathroom added an extra layer of craptastic.

Pun intended.

That fang face and his super-sized minions hadn't found me yet was a minor miracle. Hopefully, they were scouring Central Station, or better yet the international terminal. I'd gambled and chose the Sandymount Station, which was further from the Portebello neighborhood where I'd been staying, and in the opposite direction of the airport.

It had been both unrealistic and naïve to believe that whoever had proclaimed the women in my family a threat to anything other than ourselves would give me a pass.

Hiding hadn't worked for my mother, her mother, or her mother's mother. What really sucked, aside from the whole dying thing, was that I had no freaking idea why we were cursed. Either that knowledge, like an old photograph had faded with time, or the reason we'd been cursed was so foul no one wanted to give voice to the offense. Maybe I was as evil as so many people have said throughout my life.

But that was a them problem, not a Gwen problem. I'd grown accustomed to living—thank you very much—and planned to do it a whole lot longer.

I stretched my arms upward, then out to the side before checking the massive white industrial clock on the other side of the terminal.

Four forty-five. Fifteen minutes until the first northbound train.

The new plan was shaky, bordering on foolish. First, I decided to head in the opposite direction of the airport. From there, I'd regroup, and arrange for a ferry, flight, or freaking swim. All I needed to do was make it another day.

My knees snapped, crackled, and popped as I lumbered from the floor. Then ignoring the aches and pains, I trudged toward the platform, anxiety munching on my stomach lining. I suspected if I made it through the next twenty-four hours, it wouldn't be without an ulcer.

A group of ten or so laughing backpackers entered the side entrance, so I walked beside them twenty feet or so then slipped into the riptide of commuters. Like a school of fish, everyone swam with the current, splitting off at a stairwell, the gap quickly filled by another reluctant worker.

When I finally reached the platform, I scoped out the crowd. Some, like little soldiers, stood on the yellow painted lines to queue up for the train; while others leaned against the tan tile walls, uneager to begin the day's labor. As I walked down the platform, lips moving in silent prayer, I psychically put out feelers for the not quite human.

Only then, for the first time since I'd left the B&B, I smiled.

Typically, I made it my mission to take up as much space as possible. The world worked hard enough to make me feel small, invisible, and less than. This morning, however, I had to go along for the ride. I sat on the bench, squeezing between a yawning businessman and a couple who looked like they'd just rolled out of bed.

Too bad for the rest of us they'd used stale beer and cigarettes for their morning toilette. Which was convenient, since many creatures hunted by scent, and I had no idea what was stalking me.

I leaned back, slipping my hands into my jacket pockets. In my right, I fingered the cool handle of the knife I pinched from the kitchen. In my left, I traced the sharp edge of a business card.

It was black, glossy, and holy crap, made of metal. A normal person's name would emblazon the front. But not the fancy Mr. Ash Modeus. No name, no email, nothing but a phone number in etched gold letters. Since I'd deprived myself the pleasure of touching the man, I gently glided my finger across the taunting numbers. I sucked in a tiny breath as a familiar trill of masculine energy zipped straight from my fingertips to my lady bits.

I snatched my hand away.

Ash.

The only human I'd ever encountered with will rivaling the undead.

My stomach sank at a realization. Ash may be the only human in Ireland capable of hiding me from the vampire and his toadies. Murdering someone as connected as Ash wouldn't be good—for anyone.

"Miss Carter?" Ash's rumbly voice sounded surprised.

"Yes, one and the same." I sat up straight looking around the platform like he might appear from a wisp of smoke. "Sorry for calling you at this ungodly hour."

"Not a problem."

I hesitated, did I really want to do this, to place myself in a vulnerable situation with a stranger? I've accomplished a lot in my short life professionally, but personally, my greatest achievement was that I'd managed to remain both alive and safe without help from anyone.

After the events of the last few hours, it was clear that was no longer the case. I needed a hand—and protection. And right now, Ash was the biggest baddest kid in the sandbox, and I wanted him at my side. Or rather, at my back.

He seemed the type of man who surrounded himself with armed minions. I loved that word; it didn't get used enough outside of comic books.

Yes, I'd crafted a plan, but even I knew it to be a bad one, and perhaps even impossible without a little help. Holing up in Ash's house, working, and getting paid to do it sounded like a win.

"Miss Carter." Ash's rumbly voice steered me back to my ugly reality.

"Sorry," I mumbled over what I imagined to be rustling silk sheets in the background, which of course, sent my mind straight to the gutter. "I'm available now. Did you still want a piece of me?" I blurted.

Ash chuckled, and the phone damned near ignited.

"That came out wrong." I glanced over at the businessman who was full-on eavesdropping. Seriously what was with these people?

"Where should my driver collect you?" Ash asked, sounding more awake and still sexy.

"I'm getting on the train to Greystones."

He grunted. "Actually, that's convenient. Would you mind traveling outside of Ireland?"

Whether it was common sense, or good old-fashioned skepticism, I hesitated. It didn't take a rocket scientist to know that when something seemed too good to be true, it usually was.

"Miss Carter?" Ash's voice pulled me from falling down the rabbit hole of what ifs.

I cleared my throat. "Oh, sorry, I—"

The overhead speaker crackled. Then a garbled announcement blared as the train rumbled and squealed to a stop.

"Hold on a sec, my train's here. If we get cut off, I'll call right back."

The couple next to me were now sound asleep. I started to walk away and leave their drunk asses there. Instead, I stopped, kicked the guy's foot, then jabbed my thumb toward the train.

My job was done. Hopefully the good deed racked up some karma points.

I slid my phone into my pocket and filed onboard, stopping at the first set of open seats, which happened to be a group of four.

I tossed my backpack next to the window, and settled in, placing the square toolkit on my lap, before slipping my phone from my pocket. "Sorry about that Ash, what were you saying?" I slid lower on the hard plastic seat, watching passengers juggle their coffee cups, purses, and phones as they hustled for the perfect spot.

"My plans have also taken an unexpected turn. I must return home. However, you may create your masterpiece in the evenings, and explore, shop, or just lounge by the pool during the day."

Okay, this could be a good thing. I slid my jaw back and forth; thankful I hadn't snapped any teeth these last few hours. "I could use a tan. Where's home?"

"Morocco. We'd be landing in a small airport outside of Marrakesh."

My blossoming smile turned into a grimace. This was too easy, too perfect, something had to go wrong. "What about visas? Do I need one?"

"No." His tone said that clearly, only his rules mattered. Which would be cool if it were his ass getting tossed in a foreign prison. "I'll collect you at the Bray station."

"Hold your horses, Bubba. Leaving the country with a stranger wasn't on the bingo card." I glanced out the window to the opposite track and my heart screeched to a halt. There, standing on the opposite platform was the massive man from the alley. Seriously? What the hell? Did I have a giant kill me sign flashing over my head?

Not only was he there, but he stared at me as his finger moved over the screen of his smartphone.

"Miss Carter, you'll be perfectly safe." Ash sounded so reasonable using that voice usually reserved for coaxing terrified children from beneath the bed.

The beast across the tracks winked. Yikes, that was all kinds of wrong, for too many reasons to list.

"Okay fine. I'll go," I said to Ash, sounding a little too breathy. "That would be great," I mumbled, unable to stop thinking about that movie, Midnight Express. Maybe the monsters would be the better choice. "The Bray Station," I whispered. "See you there."

"Until then," he said, then ended the call.

What in the world was I doing? Oh, I know stepping out of the fire into the flames of hell.

Finally, the train moved.

A girl, who was too blonde, too pretty, and too damned perky, grabbed the pole then pointed at the vacant seats in front of me. I quickly scanned her to make sure she was human, then nodded.

I'd spotted the young lady with her oversized backpack in the station when I'd arrived. Trust, if I hadn't been on the run, no way in the world would I have spent the night anywhere but a bed. I was too old for that roughing it life.

"Sleeping in stations sucks," the young woman said as she squeezed past. When I gave her the Black woman eyebrow she quickly added, "Not that I was stalking you or anything."

I gave her a closed mouth half-assed smile before returning my hand to my pocket, stroking the knife handle like a talisman. What was I planning to do, shank the woman for being friendly? I wasn't that big of a bitch—not even to morning people.

My perky little seatmate set her supersized backpack on the floor, stretching her legs out using it as a footstool. "American?" she asked

I shrugged. "I'm not sure whether I should answer that question." I smiled a little to remove the sharp edge from my words. "How about you?"

The young woman's broad open smile made me feel bad about being judgy—almost. "Kentucky."

She seemed harmless enough, and she was definitely human. Plus, Kentucky wasn't the first fellow solo traveler I'd encountered who hungered for conversation. So, I nodded, then sort of answered her question. "Fellow country girl here."

"You don't have much of an accent."

I laughed. "I haven't lived there for a long time." *Too long.*

No matter how twisted and effed up, Hoodoo, Texas, was my Cheers, where everyone knew my name. Most importantly, they knew the real me and loved me anyway. The freaking idiots.

Kentucky put one of her earbuds in, yawning as she crossed her arms, tucking her hands in her armpits. "Are you going to be on awhile?" After I nodded, she added, "Would you mind waking me before you get off? I want to be half-way coherent when I meet my boyfriend and his relatives in Greystones."

"Not a problem, my stop is near the end, so I got you."

"Thanks," she said before popping the other earbud in and leaning her head against the window.

With each stop further away from Dublin, the car emptied. People entered the train, but even more left. Before I forgot, I shot off a quick text to my bestie Kyle including a picture of Ash's business card, along with the instructions that if he hasn't heard from me in twenty-four hours to notify my family. Needless to say, Kyle wasn't happy about not knowing where I was headed, but he'd get over it.

Yay me. I managed to make it most of the ride without having a panic attack. At least until three stations before my stop, when a man the size of a pickup truck entered the car. Okay, that's fine. Big dudes needed to catch the train too. I had almost convinced myself that I was participating in size shaming when he stopped moving.

Unlike the smart people on the train, I didn't avert my eyes, afraid to attract the hungry predator's attention. I'd rather see the bus coming.

His gaze met mine—and held.

And held.

Then freaking held some more.

Finally, he nodded, and it *wasn't* the international hey-fellow-Black-person gesture.

Of course not. It was a whole lot scarier, reminding me of the man from behind the B&B. But that wasn't it either. This man felt evil, like in an I'd-like-to-see-you-without-your-skin kind of way. Some people no matter how pretty the face, couldn't hide the menace.

If evil was a coin with two faces, Ash's would be the neutral evil side. I didn't know the man, but he seemed like a the-ends-justifies-the-means kind of guy. While this dude looked like he'd torch the world and laugh.

In other words, I'd rather deal with the vampire, because human monsters were the worst.

I raised my chin, not bothering with the whole fake smile thing. And without missing a beat, he nodded, and his full lips curved up on one side. But those eyes no matter how beautiful a brown, remained dead. Dude had a face only the grim reaper would love.

He took a seat five rows away. Of course, facing my direction. *Great.*

I wasn't sure if it was heartburn or a heart attack, but my chest was on fire. Thank heavens he was merely a supersized human, so he couldn't smell my terror. And couldn't see it either, thanks to years of perfecting my resting bitch face.

Normally, I didn't live in the world of maybes, but today I moved right the hell in. Maybe big scary dude wasn't on the train for me. Maybe the frightening man commuted to work and had a perfectly boring job as a real estate agent or banker. But the way he watched me said something else. Something terrible. Something I'd ignore—at least for the moment.

"Next stop Bray," a tinny female voice said over the intercom, dragging me from my doom spiral.

I shifted in my seat, glancing out the window at the lush green countryside.

The landscape made me want to wiggle my toes in the living carpet of dense grass. Would the hills soon be covered by wildflowers or groomed by flocks of sheep?

Someday I'd love to learn the answer in real time. Should I live long enough.

Kentucky had been serious about getting her sleep on, judging by the drool escaping the corner of her mouth.

The train slowed, and people lumbered from their seats, queuing up to leave. I grabbed my backpack, first sliding my arms through the straps and tightening them down. As I leaned over to wake Miss Kentucky, I peered through the crowd.

Shit.

At some point on the ride, I'd managed to block out scary dude, and imagined myself a regular woman enjoying a solo holiday. While I wasn't exactly a worrier by nature, I tended to not get my panties in a wad about crap I couldn't control. In retrospect, that probably wasn't a good idea. Especially not today.

Because if I'd been paying attention, I'd have noticed that instead of one scary bus in a suit, two friends had joined him. And the cherry on top of the shit sundae? The Three Stooges of bone breaking stared at me through gaps in the crowd. Wasn't I the lucky one?

The train squealed to a stop, and I shook Kentucky's shoulder before shifting my knees toward the aisle and tightening my death grip on the handle of my case.

A ruddy cheeked man-child wearing a Manchester United jacket, stopped, motioning for me to enter the fray.

"Thank you." I slipped out, body slumped and head down. If the three stooges were after me, the best I could hope for was they'd be slow. Then again, I could also be kind of full of myself. Maybe they were merely stunned by my beauty.

Yeah, right.

I slipped off the train, keeping up with the morning crowd. As I turned the corner for the exit, I looked behind me and saw… nothing. What was that saying about hammers and nails? Something about if your only tool was a hammer, blah, blah, blah. Apparently, not everyone was out to kill me.

Once I stepped into the brisk April morning, I hurried down the escalator and out the station. As I slipped my cell from my pocket, a sleek charcoal gray Maybach turned the corner.

Wow, talk about a sexy beast.

"Hey Texas," a familiar female voice called out behind me.

I spun around, frowned, then shook my head. "This wasn't your stop."

"I know, just wanted to give you my number. If you're going to be here awhile, we should hook up to share a pint. Just in case I need an escape." Kentucky's smile was bright, but something was different. Even with her overloaded backpack, she moved with a dancer's grace. And her eyes…

They were shrewd, hard, and too alert for a woman who'd allegedly slept the last thirty minutes.

I shifted my kit to my right hand, spread my legs, distributing my weight evenly, then smiled and put on my I'm-too-stupid-to-live expression. "That sounds like a great idea."

"What's your number? I'll text you mine." Kentucky stopped in front of me and slipped her hand in the pocket of her bright yellow waterproof jacket. When her hand reappeared, between her pale fingers wasn't a phone, or even a damned ink pen, but a small .380.

All my self-defense training kicked in at once. Simultaneously, I knocked the hand holding the gun down and away from me as I shifted to the side, blading my body. Using momentum and good old gravity, I shifted and swung my right arm. Then all fifteen pounds of my kit smashed against the side of her head.

See, there was a reason I've never trusted morning people.

The Maybach skidded to a halt and the back door flew open. I kicked the still spinning pistol toward the gutter, where it teetered on a metal grate for a few seconds before it disappeared.

My heart thumped, in a combination of self-recrimination and pissed the eff off.

Not only was I an idiot, but sexist. I'd been so focused on the men; I'd ignored the threat sitting right next to me. But in my defense, what self-respecting assassin drooled? That had to be against the code.

If not, it should be.

I dashed to the waiting car and slid inside like I was headed for home plate. Luckily, the driver's sense of urgency matched my own. She sped off before my door thumped closed.

Now that was my kind of woman.

The car was silent. No music, no breathing, no nothing. Not even the ambient outside noise dared intrude. I exhaled once, twice, then a third time before opening my eyes and divesting myself of my backpack.

That was way too close.

I plastered a smile on my face and shifted, expecting to see a man reconsidering spending time alone with a violent, crazy-ass, Black woman.

But once again, Mr. Ash Modeus surprised me. For there he sat, wearing Ireland's biggest shit-eating grin.

The responding butterflies banging in my tummy had nothing to do with a near death experience and everything to do with my traveling companion.

Maybe, just maybe, I could learn to like this man.

Chapter 5

Ash and I stepped onto the tarmac at the small Moroccan airport, and I scanned the area. Honestly, I didn't expect to find anything this far from civilization, but a woman couldn't be too careful.

No ghosts, no ghouls, no fae. Nothing but ordinary humans.

Even with uncertainty swirling around me, that first spark of hope flickered in my heart, and before I could help myself, I grinned. It didn't take but a few seconds for that grin to turn into a smile and some of the tension in my neck eased.

"I take it you approve?" Ash looked down at me. The lines of his face hadn't changed, and the square jaw and unsmiling lips were as harsh as when I'd met him last night. But I bet there was laughter dancing in those dark brown eyes, I just couldn't see them beneath the mirrored shades.

"Absolutely," I said, wishing I had sunglasses to hide behind.

It wasn't Ash's car, the sleek private plane, or even his dark good looks and impeccable manners that impressed me. But whisking us through Moroccan customs at the small airport in less than ten minutes without having to speak with anyone was nothing short of a minor miracle.

Oh, and that he hadn't asked about my little train station boxing match was priceless.

A driver waited next to a gleaming black Mercedes. He, like Ash, was dressed in the dangerous man uniform of dark glasses and an impeccably tailored suit. And, like Ash, had that same aura of invincibility and too much... something jammed into too small a body.

"Choukran," I said to the driver as I slid in the back of the waiting car.

The driver nodded, not bothering to hide his surprise.

"You speak Arabic?" Ash asked as soon as the door closed behind him.

"Not even a little." I snapped my seatbelt closed and shrugged. "Google is my friend. I learned a long time ago that a smile and learning the basics is the least I can do as a visitor."

"Are you sure you're American?"

"We're not all heathens."

The trunk closed with a soft thunk. A second man double tapped the roof, then the third leg of my journey began.

"That's good to know," Ash said with what could be mistaken as humor. "I have been a most negligent host. I spent the entirety of the flight conducting business."

"Don't apologize for working. This isn't a date. And speaking of business, we need to discuss your tattoo."

He flicked his fingers as if batting away the idea of something so frivolous. Hey, it was his money—and his ass should my enemies find me. "Is this your first visit to Morocco?" Ash asked.

"Unfortunately, yes. Africa has been at the top of the bucket list for a while."

"I must ensure you make time to see it."

I looked at him for a few seconds. Let's see... for some reason, this man was paying me a shit ton of money, saving me from assassins, and was tossing in some sightseeing on top of it?

I'd be foolish to say no. "That would be cool." I sank into the soft leather seat the same black as the exterior, sighed, then smiled at Ash. "Thank you."

"I've waited a long time for you." He shifted slightly and crossed his arms, studying me for a few seconds before speaking. "You never answered my question last night."

"Questions? All I heard were demands."

"Are you and Riley lovers?"

"Oh, that." I blinked, searching for the right words, which didn't include either eff or you, since the man was paying me a mint and saving my bacon. But this was also the time for boundaries. A concept which Ash apparently didn't understand.

Unlike most people, he did comprehend that he who spoke first lost. And despite knowing Ash for all of five minutes, I could tell defeat wasn't a cup his sipped from often—if ever.

"Mr. Modeus, my—"

"Ash—"

"Okay, Ash, my personal life is off limits. Got it?"

"Absolutely." His tone was solemn, but his lips twitched.

"What's so funny?"

"Your candor is...unusual." He sounded almost confused as if no was not a word tossed in his direction often.

"Most people are probably too afraid of you to talk smack."

The driver snorted, then covered it (badly) with a cough.

"I have many friends. People don't fear me. Do they Omar?"

"Did you say something, sir?" Omar met my eyes in the mirror and winked.

"Don't drag that poor man into it. Let's keep it real. People in your circles either want you, something from you, or think you'll rip their hearts out, so they're terrified."

"Which group would you fall into?"

"None of them."

Ash stared at me for a few seconds as if tasting my words.

Well, they were mostly the truth, because when it came down to it, I too wanted something from the powerful Mr. Modeus.

Protection.

His ringing phone interrupted the moment. "So you say, Miss Carter. So you say." He withdrew his cell from his jacket pocket. "Excuse me."

While Ash chatted first in French, then switching to something that sounded like Arabic, I closed my eyes, placed my hands on my thighs palms up, and sank into myself. Silence. What a glorious thing. Since Morocco was as old as civilization, I'd expected to need a horse tranquilizer to mellow myself out. But the peace that cradled my soul was so profound, I wanted to weep.

The world, the car, and even Ash disappeared. It was as if I could almost hear the ancestors welcoming me home.

When I opened my eyes, it was to Ash watching me.

"You've asked few questions." He slipped his cell into his inner jacket pocket. The way he moved; the serious way he observed my every gesture, reminded me of a jungle cat. "Did Google tell you everything you needed to know."

"Some things the internet or even our mutuals can't tell me. As a woman, I move through the world differently. Placing myself in vulnerable situations, especially with men is a calculated risk. So, I'm forced to judge you by your actions rather than your intent."

"Was this a risk worth taking?"

I hadn't been lying to Riley when I said I had a second sense about people. Ash was dangerous, and his business dealings may hop over the line to illegal, but I didn't sense I'd be in the kind of danger that would leave my body battered.

Finally, I nodded. "I'd have to say yes."

He tilted his head. "I'm glad, Miss Carter."

"Please, call me Gwen."

"If I should use your first name, I prefer Gwendolyn."

I liked the way the syllables of my name fell from his lips, so I nodded, before returning my attention to my window. This was just another job, and it would serve me well to remind myself—frequently.

We'd just passed the Chichaoua sign on the well paved freeway, surrounded by endless blue skies and unending miles of yellowish sand interrupted occasionally by wide squat trees. Rather than appearing desolate, it felt... peaceful. Ahead of us about fifty feet or so off the side of the road was another sprawling tree but this one was covered with white spots. As we pulled aside, my eyes widened.

I gasped.

Those weren't odd white blooms on those sturdy branches, but goats. "Holy, crap," I whispered, probably sounding like a kid on Christmas morning after a generous visit from Santa. Most of the goats were white, but a couple had various amounts of black fur. The tree and especially the cute little goat with the half black face were gone too quickly. Hopefully, I'd have the chance to get some pictures of the tree beasties before I left Morocco.

Ash would have to work hard to top a goat tree. I wasn't a giggling kind of woman but the thought of someone needing a goat and plucking it from a tree made me do just that.

"You should do that more often," Ash said, his voice low.

"What?" I sat back in my seat, feeling like a kid on a school trip.

"Smile."

I bared my teeth. And when Ash laughed, the man went from handsome to stunning. Not the overly sculpted face of men in magazines. No, his attractiveness was akin to primal fear. Something that called to me on a cellular level.

"Once our business has concluded, I'll take you to on a safari. It's seems a pity to not take advantage."

"I can't make any promises. You might pluck my last nerve before then."

His lips did that twitching thing again, like he was too cool to laugh at the silly woman. "I'll do my best not to..." Ash tapped his index finger against his chin, then nodded. "Yes, pluck your nerve endings."

I chuckled.

Ash shrugged. "What is it you kids say? Just roll with it."

I laughed. "First of all, I'm not sure I was ever a kid. And you're like what? Ten years younger than me?"

"I know exactly how old you are Gwendolyn."

The way he said it made it feel so official so...like that Christmas movie, *It's a Wonderful Life*. Specifically, that part when the angel said the bit about the bells ringing and the angels getting wings.

But it wasn't wings that Ash was doling out.

Finally, Ash tore his gaze from mine and glanced down at his watch. "We should arrive in approximately ten minutes."

"I can't wait to get a good look around," I whispered reverently as I watched a lone man atop a camel in the distance. I wanted to do, see, taste, and touch everything. I could already tell that Morocco would inspire me.

"Do you have any ancestral ties to the land?"

"Don't we all?" I looked away, hoping he hadn't caught the ache I was unable to hide whenever I thought of my always silent ancestors. Not that it was a surprise to anyone, especially in a town called Hoodoo, that my family were practitioners. After my mother died, I had a new home in a new town, and was exposed to an entirely new set of beliefs.

I'd done everything right—the altars, the candles, my mother's favorite foods—and nothing. Not once did I receive a message, a sweet touch, or even a visitation in a dream. Eventually, I had to face the truth. Not only had my mother died and left me in this life, but the other one too.

To say I was a handful as a kid was an understatement. Maybe the woman just needed a break. A long one. Like... forever.

Luckily the car slowed, dragging me from my pitiful thoughts. We paused in front of a massive ornate metal gate with ten-foot stone walls on each side. The only bit of the compound visible from the car was the palm trees lining the curving driveway like soldiers.

Two men, both heavily armed stepped from the shadows, looked through the gate, nodded, then one of them punched a code in a handheld device. Only then did Omar, our driver, hit a button on the dash and the gates opened.

I smiled as the gate silently closed behind us. Because when it came to hideouts, I couldn't have created a safer place. Or I sure as hell hoped so.

Chapter 6

"Dear ancestors, this is..." My feet were barely on the ground and it was clear that Texas had a rival for my affections. Ash's home was a kaleidoscope of a compound. The explosion of blues and whites with hints of dark green should have been dizzying and overwhelming, instead it filled me with calm.

The driver left us in what looked to be a back courtyard with a small seating area tucked beneath a vine covered pergola. The large waxy leaves gave enough shade in the April afternoon, while allowing a sprinkling of sunlight to pepper the white wrought iron furniture.

With a gallant wave, Ash motioned for me to proceed into a wide tunnel, its curved ceiling and walls covered with more elaborate tiny mosaic tiles. If I thought the back courtyard was beautiful, I had no idea, and whoa, I wasn't ready.

We stepped out of the shaded area and entered paradise.

What I'd planned to do was remain sophisticated and unimpressed. But this was me we're talking about. "Daaaaammn..."

"You like?" Ash's face was a mixture of amusement and pride.

"It's okay. Better than a tent." I shrugged, then burst out laughing.

But now, with the iron gates shuttered behind me and burly well-armed men patrolling the grounds, a sister could almost taste freedom. And the best part? This joint was one hundred percent supernatural creature free.

At least so far.

A part of me ached to poke, prod, and examine how that could happen, especially in such an old building. Either a: this was a new build, or b: humans weren't the only beings Ash intimidated.

I had to go with option a, for sanity's sake.

Once again, Ash seemed to fight back a grin. "The name Ash Modeus has been connected to this piece of land since..." He nodded as if counting the years before adding, "...Forever."

I studied him intently. If twenty-first century Ash hopped in a time machine and traveled back a century or two, he'd have no problems. Standing in this sumptuous compound, I imagined Ash a warlord or someone equally dangerous and powerful. His was a body meant to wield a wicked curved sword. The image of this man rocking MC Hammer pants while slaughtering his enemies made me smile.

"I wonder how much you resemble the first Ash Modeus," I finally said before I burst into hysterical laughter.

"Some days I ponder that myself, Gwendolyn." His expression grew distant for a nanosecond before he returned to himself. "This is the favorite of my homes. It pleases me that you like it."

"I didn't say all that." We walked an entire three steps before the word vomit started up again. "You know, I'd always imagined my heaven would look like Moorea, with the white sand beaches and crystal-clear azure water. It's my favorite place on the planet." We walked beneath an overhang around a massive inner courtyard filled with plants, pottery, and water structures—including a lap pool—I looked at Ash and sighed. "I may have to reassess."

Ash's face, usually all lines and angles softened, as did his voice. "Feel free to avail yourself of any of the amenities."

"That's an offer I won't refuse."

The interior of the house was as beautiful as the outside, managing to do so without feeling ostentatious. This was a home to be lived in. To laugh and love in. To settle down and create your dreams in.

In other words, it was perfect.

Ceiling fans whirred overhead. The massive folding glass doors leading to the inner courtyard were open, making the comfortable but expansive space seem larger.

I followed Ash through the living room then up a staircase made for a Cinderella moment. Once again, I noted the understated elegance of the delicately carved banister, the vases filled with plants, and the arching fronds peeking out from beyond the balustrade.

The second story of the house was open, gifting a view of the main floor. It struck me that it also afforded time to escape your enemies once you saw them coming.

Not only was I happy to...well, you know—stay alive, exploring Ash's home during my free time would be a blast. And once I survived my doomsday. Which was...holy shit. I only needed to make it past midnight, my birthday, the day I slid screaming into the world, then my life would finally be my own. Except for disease, famine, pandemics, and the ever-approaching old age.

In other words, normal stuff.

"This is your sanctuary for as long as you choose." He paused before a set of doors large enough for three people to enter side by side.

"You're going to have to be careful with those invitations. Some women would never leave."

"It's not one I issue lightly," he said as he placed his palm against the door and pushed it open.

Had to give it to him, dude was smooth. My supernatural death sentence ended at midnight, but the whole lover dying thing...

Not so much.

As grateful as I was for the convenient escape, I'd be naive to believe my unique talents as an artist was my sole purpose in Casa del Hot Dude. Welp, Ash and I could use each other.

"The staff are at your disposal regardless of the time. Just call. The numbers are on the bedside table." He nodded, then headed down the hall.

"Ash," I called out after he'd taken a few steps. "Thank you. You're a lifesaver."

Literally.

"You're most welcome." He turned around, unbuttoning his jacket. "I'm pleased not to only share my home, but your birthday."

"My..." I narrowed my eyes. "How did you...?"

"Your passport picture is fetching." He walked backward, and his lips did that not quite a smile thing. "Forty-five will look great on you."

I dashed inside my room before I suggested something else that would look good on me.

Like him.

It was more than Ash and the seductive environment that had me up in my feelings. Seeing that I had that whole black widow thing going on, sex had been off the table for years. So, I sought my pleasure with art, shopping, and travel. But even then, the specter of my family's curse clouded my joy. Yet still, I had to remind myself that sex with me equaled death for my partner. So no seeing Ash naked outside of my dreams.

With my back pressed against the door, I grinned at the lush, not even close to gender neutral guest room. Where the rest of the home was obviously male, this space was created with feminine tastes and comfort in mind. What I wasn't going to do was overthink why he placed me in this room but enjoy it I would.

After I handled some business.

The burnt orange backpack and dented tool kit that had been my constant travel companions, sat on an old-school wood and canvas luggage rack. "You can take the girl out of the country," I muttered, ignoring the heat shooting from my chin straight to my hairline.

Not even my attitude was armor enough to wonder what the staff thought when they brought my things upstairs. Had I planned a fancy trip, I would have brought appropriate luggage—and clothes.

I huffed. "Whatever."

One peek in the mirror and I cringed. "Holy crap woman." I leaned in closer and shook my head. "Talk about rode hard and put away wet." The chick staring back at me looked exactly like someone who'd been chased by vampires, goons, and assassins. And I thought Ash was wanting some of this?

A good whiff of my pits disabused me of that idea.

First things first. I snagged the burner phone that held one number and hit call.

"Where are you?" Loretta's Texas drawl was thick with worry.

While technically my cousin, from the moment I moved to Hoodoo, Loretta became a mentor, confidant, and treasured play aunt. Her home was where I would have chosen to live, but for some unfathomable reason my mother selected a freaking vampire to be my ward.

Or should I say warden?

"Safe," I said, feeling like it was actually the truth.

"You sure?" Some of her concern had dissipated, replaced by a whopping dose of disbelief.

I put a smile in my voice and answered. "Positive." One handedly, I unraveled my large messy top bun, setting my locs free.

"I just did a reading—"

"Things were... dicey last night and even this morning. But I'm okay." My voice softened with both belief and relief. And for the first time in... forever, it was true. "I promise."

She harrumphed, then uttered a few colorful phrases.

"How is everything in good old Hoodoo?" I chuckled, glancing at the bed before plopping my behind on the cream damask bench placed at its foot. Sitting on a bed—even one I didn't own—wearing street clothes always struck me as nasty. After a night on planes, trains, and automobiles, my jeans were as germ ridden as the soles of my boots.

"Don't change the subject," Loretta snapped, her voice holding little heat.

"Would I do that?"

"Hell yeah." Loretta paused. When she spoke again, her voice was soft and laced with both warning and power. "My bones don't lie. Come home. Let your people protect you."

"No. Risking my life is one thing, Risking yours? Not going to happen." Just then, a fluffy white cloud cruised over the courtyard. "Not even I'm that evil."

"You define who you are—the hell with anyone else."

"I know." Unconsciously, I stroked the birthmark on my arm. The one my mother's fanatical pastor proclaimed was a demon mark. When the asshole started talking about an exorcism and praying away the evil, was when Mom decided it was time to return to Hoodoo. "Hey, do you know anyone who'd use me to get back at she-who-shall-not-be-named?" I giggled.

Aunt Rose and Loretta put oil and water to shame. A better comparison would be oil and fire. Yes, there was bound to be an explosion when those two women occupied a room. Far as Loretta was concerned, a vampire had no business raising anything, especially a child. Of course, she was right, but for the wrong reasons. It wasn't the bloodsucking that made my aunt a bad parental candidate, but her unyielding standards.

"Girl, with that personality, I'm sure she has an army of enemies."

"Be nice..."

"That *was* nice. Why you asking?"

I exhaled, staring at the delicate watercolor landscape that looked suspiciously like a Monet. One that went missing seventy-five years ago. Stolen art nor any of Ash's other illegal dealings were any of my damned business. And sharing my confrontation with fang face last night was none of Loretta's.

There had to be a reason for the bad blood (pun intended) between Loretta and Aunt Rose. I'd seen Loretta laugh and joke with my uncle and some of the other vamps from the Double R ranch. So whatever friction stood between Loretta and Aunt Rose was personal—and went deep.

And neither of them would share what happened. In other words, another secret tossed in the family closet.

"Who would want me dead?" I asked.

"Well... a certain witch in Hoodoo might have a motive."

I pursed my lips, shoving down the guilt and hurt rolled up with the fonder memories of my old friend. "Rita should be over that by now."

"Would you be?" Loretta asked simply, her words holding neither judgement nor rebuke. Which was good, since I judged myself harshly enough.

"Some folks hold on to grudges too long. That was what, twenty years ago?"

"Woo." Loretta cackled, and I could almost imagine her bent over, slapping her boney thigh. "I know you not talking."

I burst out laughing, and she started up again. Orneriness was an inherited trait in my family. At least Aunt Rose, the vampire, would just kill you. But Loretta, she was dangerous in a way that you'd suffer in this life and maybe even the next. Let her tell it though, she'd never put a root on anyone who didn't have it coming.

Thank goodness I stayed on her good side.

"Loretta?"

"Yeah sweetie?"

"One more day," I whispered, praying I'd live to see the moon rise on this night of my birth. One I'd celebrate with the mysterious Ash.

"That may be so, but girl be careful." Loretta sounded more hopeful, but not convinced.

"As a virgin on her wedding night. Hey, are your bones handy?"

"What do you think?"

I smiled. They were Loretta's version of an American Express Card. She never left home without them. "Would you throw them now?"

"Hold on." She shuffled around. I pictured her slippers sliding across her tile kitchen floor and her housecoat swishing against those twigs she called legs. Did she still have that green and white Formica table? I spent many a Saturday afternoon helping her snap peas and peel potatoes for the Sunday dinners at her house. Those meals were large, raucous, and loving affairs. And we won't even talk about the food.

My mouth watered just thinking about her pork chops smothered with gravy.

"You want me to throw them blind or do you have a question?" Loretta asked.

"Let me think..." I gently tugged my lower lip as I walked to the window. The universe required specificity. For instance, asking if I were in danger would probably get a quick and resounding yes. Because hey, life was dangerous.

So, I paused, closed my eyes, then slowed my thoughts.

By the time my lungs emptied, it was clear that I only needed one answer. "Will my killers follow me to Mor—" I silently cursed. "To where I am now?"

If the bones, the ancestors, or anything else wanted Loretta to know my location, they could tell her.

The low *click-clack* of the chicken bones followed by the muted skittering against the cloth made me long for Hoodoo. Not the religion, since it didn't seem to work—at least not for me—but the place. It was home whether I'd wanted it to be or not.

Loretta let out a happy squeal. "Lord have mercy. I guess I can stop worrying."

"Really?" I could barely speak through the relief bubbling through my veins like champagne. Did this mean that I can fully enjoy myself without looking over my shoulder every thirty seconds?

"Yes. Whoever was chasing you is where you left them."

"Thank you." I almost sobbed. Damn, I haven't cried since my mother's funeral. None of life's triumphs and heartbreaks had come even close. But now, standing in a desert paradise, five inches from freedom, the waterworks were ready to spring to life.

Until Loretta splashed me with a frigid bucket of reality. "Death ain't the only thing you're running from."

"I know but—"

"But nothing. Tell me you haven't been toting that deck of tarot cards I gave you for your sixteenth birthday all over God's creation?"

Have I mentioned that woman had a bloodhound's nose for lies?

If smug superiority had a tone, that's what painted Loretta's words. "Yeah, that's what I thought. Pull those cards out and listen to what they have to say."

"But it's been so long…"

"Well, just apologize and pray over them. Enough of that, I got things to do. You ain't the only one in demand missy. So, am I going to see you in three to four days?"

I loved Texas, the trees, the greenery, and call me sick—even the humidity. But something about this place, not sure if it was Morocco itself, or this part of the world. It just felt… Different.

Of course, Ash chose that very moment to walk across the courtyard, pausing beneath my balcony like a Middle Eastern Romeo. "I don't know."

On one level it was eerily like the large male in the alley last night. But the little cha-cha my lady parts did in response to the delectable Ash wasn't about fear.

"I have a feeling it may be a bit longer, but you'll have plenty of notice. Get the Boudin and barbecue ready."

"Deal. Now you go on and have yourself some fun," Loretta hissed. "Gwen, I don't know what this means, but the bones say that you don't have to worry about that other curse as long as you're wherever you are. Does that make sense?"

My eyelids did a morse code impression. I mean, that would be cool and all if the suave Mr. Modeus was interested. "Are you sure?" I asked wrapping my arm around my waist.

"About as much as I can be."

Which meant yes. Because in all the years I've known Loretta, she'd never been wrong. I sure as hell hope this won't be the first time.

Chapter 7

There were few things on this side of the grave better than a hot shower and clean hair. Standing in a bathroom fit for a queen, I unwrapped my locs, tossed the damp towel in the hamper, and rewrapped it with another.

Steam and the heady scent of citrus with undernotes of vanilla and something else filled the air of a bathroom the size of a large suburban bedroom. My visit might be brief, but I had every intention of getting well acquainted with that sunken tub.

I cupped my hands over my nose and mouth. What kind of magic was in that lotion? Seriously, I was absolutely, positively in love. Come on? What was not to like about a man who understood the importance of moisturizer?

And did I mention the hair products?

Either Ash, or the mistress of moisture on his staff, was absolutely going on Santa's nice list.

But as much as I could live in the bathroom, I should probably get dressed.

I sighed, tightened the belt on my robe, then reluctantly left my private sanctuary.

"Now, you and I can get properly acquainted," I said to the large bed with a gauzy white mosquito netting. "Alright Mr. Ash Modeus, that bed is almost as tempting as you are. Good job."

Each time I said his name, something tickled the back of my mind. But like a wisp of smoke, each time I reached for it, the memory dissipated.

I flopped down on the bed, sinking into the soft duvet and feather mattress beneath it. Oh yeah, this was going to be the best work vacation ever. You know, if I managed to live until tomorrow. To be on the safe side, I won't count myself free until five-thirty-seven, one minute past the time of my momentous arrival in the world. Only then, would I be truly free.

A soft knock sounded at the door.

"Crap." I'd like to believe I leapt gracefully from the bed, but why lie? It was more like a roll and bounce and grunt. I glanced down to make sure the girls hadn't exploded from the robe, then walked over to the door.

Before my fingers grazed the knob, I knew who stood on the other side.

I opened it and... whew.

Jean clad Ash was hot, business suit Ash was intimidating, but this Ash, still sweaty with a towel around his neck and t-shirt clinging to his chest was criminally seductive.

And I had a snowball's chance in hell of tapping that. You know... if I were in the market for a booty call.

My hands flittered to the towel wrapped around my hair. Yeah, not exactly sexy, but who the hell was I kidding?

I'll take realistic for a hundred, Alex.

Ash's lips twitched.

"Please tell me I did not say that out loud." My libido needed to hop off the express train to the gutter.

"Say what?"

I ignored his chuckle and crossed my arms under the breasts that without a bra could now be classified as 38 longs. Some things about aging weren't so great.

"I'm glad I caught you before you dressed, may I come in?" he asked. "When I narrowed my eyes, he chuckled. "Or I can wait a couple of minutes for you to put something else on."

"That's fine." Hell, I was already in his house in the middle of nowhere. Didn't get much more vulnerable than that. And I hated it. I didn't do helpless or scared well, it made me bitchy. Or should I say bitchier than normal?

I pulled the door open and stepped aside, making a mental note to grab a knife, seeing that I'd ditched mine in Ireland. Hey, Ash was hot and all, but I'd shank his ass if he tried any funny business. Or at least try to.

He cleared his throat as he walked passed.

Wait, could he read my mind? Because I know I didn't say that shit out loud. Just to check, I thought at him: I want to ride your Lawrence of Arabia looking ass like a pony.

He turned around, placing his hands behind his back, bringing to mind a sweaty soldier at parade rest. Only this soldier was laughing on the inside—at me. But his face remained stern, forcing me to promote him from soldier to general. "Are you finding everything to your satisfaction?" he asked before I accused him of being clairvoyant, followed by him tossing the weirdo from his house.

I pressed my lips together and shook my head. "To be honest..." I grinned, unable to contain my joy. It wasn't just the room. I never knew free tasted so damned sweet. "You sir..." I walked to the small ornate table by the door, trailing my finger along a shiny green leaf the size of my head, "...May have to serve an eviction notice. As a matter of fact, this may be the slowest tattoo in history." The painting I'd been admiring hung right in front of me. The strokes, the colors, the everything was immensely masterful. And the signature...

I've known the man less than twenty-four hours, but Ash struck me as someone who'd never sully his home with anything less than the best. Which left only one conclusion. I cleared my throat, and blinked once, twice, then a third time. Holy guacamole, Ash owned the missing Monet.

A deep bark of a chuckle from behind me made me jump. "Beautiful, isn't it?" Ash asked, his voice damned near a purr.

My fingers itched to touch the priceless canvas, which would be more criminal than its theft. One last glance at the masterpiece, then I turned and faced another.

Crossroads held not only power, but danger. Now I stood in the center of such a place. But let's keep it real, I was no collector of stolen art, but nor was I an angel. Heck, some would say I belonged in the other place.

"Miss Carter?"

I raised my chin. "The colonizers have stolen so much from so many; turnabout is delicious. Wouldn't you say?"

"I would. Your appreciation of art was why I chose this room for you."

"Thanks, but don't you fear me calling Interpol?"

"Would you?"

"No," I said, my words ringing with the truth. "This woman knows which secrets are meant to be kept."

"Do you fear nothing, Gwendolyn?"

I harrumphed, sounding too much like Loretta. "My every waking hour for I don't know how long, has been spent in abject terror."

"Yet you lived."

"Why not? It's the best revenge, so they say." I grinned, because, now dying wasn't what scared me. "Plus, I'm not a hide in the closet kind of woman."

Ash watched me for a few beats, then nodded in what appeared to be approval. "Speaking of closets, have you looked in yours?"

"Hello...I haven't seen anything past that incredible bathroom." It was too late to hide my bumpkin roots. Plus, I didn't want to.

His lips quirked. "Miss... Gwendolyn. How are you feeling?"

"Amazing." *And like I've finally outwitted and outsmarted my enemies.* "What's up?"

"Then I'd like to take you somewhere."

"Sure." I nodded. I could sleep when I'm dead. Since according to Loretta, wouldn't be anytime soon, so an adventure sounded right up my alley. "We still haven't discussed your tattoo."

"We'll have plenty of time. Tomorrow is for work; this day is for pleasure. Excuse me." He turned and headed for what I suspected was the closet. "Stay there."

I saluted. Obedience wasn't my strong suit, but I was nothing if not flexible. Rather than watch him, I glanced at the wide balcony. That would be a great place to sit and savor the view, especially with a cocktail. It felt so good to be able to breathe again.

When Ash returned, he paused with both hands behind him. "Left, or right?"

"Right."

He pulled a matte black shopping bag from behind his back. "For you, an early birthday present." When I hesitated, he continued. "A gift, go ahead."

I took the bag from his long perfect fingers and my arm dipped with its weight.

"Whoa, are you some kind of magician?" I whispered as I withdrew something far more valuable to me than that Monet—a bottle of Pappy Van Winkle.

The bottle of liquid gold in my grubby hands was considered the world's finest bourbon. The only way to get a bottle was to pay an exuberant amount for what should only cost about a hundred dollars or so, or to go to Franklin, Kentucky for the tiniest chance of entering a lottery.

In other words, the shit was damned near unobtainable. But worth the trouble.

"This bourbon is... People sell their soul for this stuff."

Ash shrugged, like it was no big deal. "That's an unwise bargain."

"You've met them. People are foolish." I tossed the empty bag on the bed. "My soul may be dark and tainted, but it's mine. I'll not be giving it up for a bottle of bourbon, no matter how tasty."

"Wise as well as beautiful. Deals with demons never work out to your advantage. The house always wins."

The skin on my arms pebbled. Was it weird that the existence of the fae, shifters, vampires, and freaking ghosts were normal, but the thought of demons walking around freaked me out?

Probably.

As far as I was concerned, demons should stay where they belonged—in hell and Washington, D.C.

"So, what should I wear on this surprise outing?" I asked as I placed my bottle of Pappy's on the side table before I tossed Ash out of my room and went full Sméagol—that little weird guy from the Hobbit—on him.

He motioned toward the closet with one hand and made a come-with-me gesture with the other. "If you'd please."

Once again, Ash headed for the closet. With a butt like that, I'd followed him almost anywhere. Hey, just because I thought the man dangerous didn't mean I couldn't appreciate all that sexy goodness. Tigers were fascinating in a way that bunnies weren't. Perhaps I was just a tiger kind of woman after all.

Behind the double doors was a space most clothes hounds *would* sell their wicked souls for.

I stepped inside and gasped.

Seriously, it was the kind of reveal that should have come with a soundtrack. The long room was about the size of the bathroom. In other words—it was massive.

A built-in dresser and fainting couch covered in what looked like the softest of velvet ever created, sat in the middle. Would it be considered cheating if I spent every spare moment in Barbie's dream closet rather than the bathroom?

"What do you think?" he asked. When I just blinked, Ash's lips did that twitching thing. "Finally, something that renders the unflappable Gwendolyn speechless."

"Oh, I'm quite flappable. I'd just rather not expose my soft underbelly. That's the best way to get got."

"That sounds exhausting."

I turned away and mumbled, "You have no idea."

One wall was filled with dresses, both short and long, some beaded and bedazzled, others not. I moved right past the shelves of folded clothes and headed straight for the boots. My therapist would say that I'd replaced sex with a boot addiction. Well, if that was the case, I was about to have a bootgasm.

I caressed a blue pointed toe. There was an art to boot making. Too soft and you're looking at ripped leather. And the stiff cheap ones...not even worth it. But to quote my girl Goldilocks, this pair was just right.

Once the leather induced endorphins faded, I shook myself.

"Wait." I spun around, clutching a boot like a weapon. "Exactly how long do you think I'm staying?"

This was the point where I should call the embassy and run screaming into the desert, but it sure as hell wouldn't be without these boots. So, I nabbed the second one—just in case.

"Forever if you want." The smile on his handsome face was more humor than I'm-going-to-lock-you-up-and-make-you-my-sex-slave.

Pity.

"Don't push it buddy." I put my fist on my not so small hips. "I'd suggest you keep in mind that I know how to skin and gut a deer."

"Duly noted. One wouldn't want to end up like poor Bambi's mother."

Okay, dude got extra points for cartoon trivia.

"I vow to be on my best behavior." He began pulling clothes off the shelves. "Today is casual, wear something comfortable."

While he went about his control freak business, I placed the dresses and other items on hangers. I pulled a vintage late 1940's orange dress from the collection, pressed it against my front, and sighed. "How did you do all this? I called you less than twelve hours ago."

Ash left the closet with an arm filled with clothes. "Worried?"

"Hello... I'm in the middle of nowhere with a man I don't know. Excuse the hell out of me for not falling at your feet."

Ash made a sound of frustration. "Were it that easy, Miss Carter."

Oh. We'd returned to formalities. Now this, was the real Ash. I didn't give a shit how much money, fame, or power anyone had. There was the face we showed the public, the one we shared with family, and the most important, the truest face was the one we exposed to ourselves. For the first time since I'd met Ash, he'd given me a peek behind the curtain.

"Because I, realize your value." He laid the clothing on the bed like my personal gun running valet, then turned to face me. "To answer your question—I began to prepare in earnest a year ago."

I blinked, studying Ash, slipping into my resting bitch face. When I didn't respond he added, "Does that frighten you?" His expression remained neutral, but a hint of challenge remained in those obsidian eyes.

A slow evil kind of amusement tugged my lips up at the corners. "No Ash, it doesn't. I'm the best. But pro tip? The closet filled with clothes and shoes my size, my favorite kind of bourbon, and all this..." I waved my arm, motioning to the rest of the room, "...is flattering but creepy in a you-plan-to-make-a-suit-out-of-my-skin kind of way. Here's a quick tip. Not the way to most women's hearts."

"You, however, are not most women." His voice was so smooth and persuasive, I could envision him standing before a jury. Hell, he almost had me convinced that I was the odd one for questioning his generosity.

"That would be true. Because *things* don't impress me. I have my own money, and it's more than enough. Texas may be all kinds of weird, but it's not a third world country, and I grew up on one of the largest ranches in the state."

"And your point?" His expression was bland, almost bored, but his voice held a trace of humor at my agitation.

And yes, I was more agitated than intimidated.

"Hold your horses, I'm getting there." I put my hands on my hips. "I need you to be really clear. You're hot and all, but that doesn't cloud my judgment. My people know exactly where I am, and when I say they take revenge to the next level, that's an understatement. So, unless you want a bunch of pissed off Texans rolling up on you..." I shrugged, almost giddy at the image of a bunch of vampires and shotgun toting root workers making their way to the desert.

He gave me the tiniest of nods. "Lovely speech. Your beloved family can save themselves the trouble. Your soul, as well as the rest of you is safe."

"Good." So said the spider to the fly. I moved closer to the clothes he's set down. "So, what do we have there?"

On the bed, he'd spread two long gauzy gowns, one with a hood, the other without, and a scarf, which I assumed was to wrap around my head. Next to it rested a pair of long khaki cargo shorts, a white linen shirt, and a hat. Okay, not too bad.

"Not to sound like a bumpkin, but what's acceptable dress here?" I asked.

"Behind these walls, whatever makes you comfortable." He chuckled at my smirk.

"That's cool, but I'd rather not walk around Marrakesh, unintentionally looking like a hooker."

That urbane veneer slipped and he gave me not the suave chuckle, or the sexy lip twitch, but a full-body laugh from his eyes down to his sneaker covered feet laugh. If I was Eve, a relaxed an amused Ash was a giant apple I wouldn't mind taking a bite from.

Once the chuckles slowed, he answered, "In that case, longer tops over your jeans, as well as shoulders and elbows covered. Head wraps aren't necessary unless you enter a mosque."

"Cool. Thank you." I loved visiting churches and houses of worship. The more ornate the better. I tilted my head and stared at Ash. He didn't seem like a bowing his head kind of guy. I picked up the cream-colored caftan thingy, rubbing the cotton fabric between my thumb and forefinger. It was softer and far lighter than it looked.

"That's called a djellaba."

"It's pretty in a Mrs. Roper kind of way." I returned it to the bed.

"Do you enjoy swimming?"

"What?" I slapped my hand against my chest and gasped. "You don't already know?"

"Of course, I'm merely being polite. Did it not work?" His frown was as fake as my surprise.

I snort laughed, then shook my head. "Not even close. But I do applaud the effort."

"There are some bathing costumes in the closet."

Whoa, when was the last time anyone called a bathing suit a costume, 1880?

Ash retrieved a black rectangular box from the nightstand. One that hadn't been there earlier. "I wish for you to let your guard down. To do that, you must be comfortable. And to be comfortable, you must feel safe. Which is why I have given this to you."

I nodded and accepted.

"Was there anything else you needed?" he asked.

Like what, an orgasm, world peace, for the assassin not to find me a minute before seven thirty-five? All of that would be nice. Instead, I just shook my head.

When he reached the door, I called out, "Ash, you're a life saver."

"Yours is a life worth saving," he said before closing the door softly behind him.

Okay... That was good to know.

I flipped open the box and smiled. Ash was a man who knew the way to my wicked heart: boots, bourbon, and a loaded 9mm.

Chapter 8

There was a reason kids squealed in delight as they zipped down steep hills on their sleds or begged their parents for swings shaded by giant ancient trees. Riding through the desert in Ash's open Range Rover reminded me of the joys of the wind against my face.

I closed my eyes, threw my arms in the air, and let out a loud whoop as we crested a ginormous sand dune and went airborne. It shouldn't have come as a surprise that an outing with Ash would be extraordinary.

After I had selected the hooded peach djellaba, I went downstairs to a smug and similarly dressed Ash. Except his outfit wasn't peach, but a manly cream with brown stripes. He then whisked me off to a private hangar. Only there was no pilot waiting.

Mr. Modeus was a man of many talents, including piloting an airplane.

Right now, zipping through the desert, I forgot everything I thought I knew and believed I liked. The massive red sand dunes of the Sahara were straight out of a movie. We're talking vistas complete with Bedouins tending their flocks, a man guiding a row of obedient camels, and miles of nothing but sunshine and cloudless skies.

In other words, fucking awesome.

Ash unwrapped the covering from his mouth and yelled, "I take it you approve?"

I'd given up trying not to eat dust ten miles earlier, so my face was uncovered and getting the world's best exfoliation thanks to the fine sand. "This is better than sex!" I considered being embarrassed for an entire nanosecond, then leaned my head back and cackled with glee.

"Then you haven't been doing it right."

While I may not be able to see his eyes behind those mirrored shades, if I had to bet, there'd be gentle mocking and a whole lot of cockiness in them. Rather than answer, I did my best adolescent imitation and poked my tongue out.

In response, Ash laughed and drove faster.

I used to scoff at those taken by the sheik books for a myriad of reasons, including fetishism, stereotypes, and good old-fashioned racism. But right now, watching Ash had me planning a trip to the library.

"Where are we going?" I asked.

"If I told you, it wouldn't be a surprise, now would it?"

"Technically yes, since I've never been there anyway."

"Nope. Those are the rules." He dipped his head down, looking at me over his glasses.

"Well, I don't like rules. You equated them with sheep, remember?"

"As well I did." He slowed and veered right, headed for what looked like a giant barren mesa. "How many would you like to break today?"

I stared at the approaching wall of rock. Was he talking about rules or bones? I'd forever been the lonely person surrounded by the laughing crowd, unable to be a true friend because there were parts of my life that must remain hidden. Outside of Hoodoo, I could never fully trust or confide in anyone.

And inside of Hoodoo...

Well, let's just say I had a butt-load of fences to mend.

But today wasn't about the past, or even the future. I needed to live in the right now. My mother had spent so much time running, wasted so much time hiding from her demons, and her grief over the death of my father, that she'd no life outside of me.

I vowed long ago to not be that woman. But somehow, even amid my career success, I'd failed. I grabbed the leather oh-shit strap and stared out my window, smiling at the row of resting camels and the man who didn't look pleased that they'd decided to have a sit down.

Those poor camels were me—freaking tired.

I turned to the waiting Ash and yelled over the rushing wind, "All of them."

"Good." He cranked up the stereo, increasing the volume of the traditional Moroccan music until it complemented the warm Saharan wind. Then he floored it.

That whole being brave and breaking the rules crap was for the birds. My butthole puckered at the impending collision with the mesa. The fact that he appeared to have no intention of slowing down or turning wasn't helping things.

"Ash..." I slammed my left hand on the dashboard and tightened my grip on the leather strap.

"Do you trust me?" he yelled.

"Um no. Please stop. I'd like to live to see my birthday."

"You will, I give you my solemn vow."

"And if you're wrong?" I glanced at the wall of jagged rock, pressed my back against the seat, then pictured my mangled and bloody body scattered amongst the wreckage.

"There will be no dying today. If you leave this earth, I will drag you back," he yelled.

"You'll be dragging me nowhere, since you'll be just as dead." The wall got closer, and I glared at Ash. "If I die, I'll hunt your ass down and make your afterlife hell."

"Promise?" He grinned, then pointed out the front window. "Watch."

We were three feet away from the wall—and death. This sucked giant monkey balls. Why would I believe that I, Gwendolyn Diane Carter, would experience my own minor miracle? Well, once again, I was ab-so-fucking-lutely wrong.

I squeezed my eyes shut, not wanting to see the end. Plus, this way I could have the dignity of not peeing my pants before I died.

Like that was some mercy.

"You're not dying today, Miss Carter," he said before coming to a whooshing, fishtailing stop that would have made Indiana Jones proud.

Eyes still closed, I patted my face, my arms, my legs and yes, even my boobs. We weren't dead. My stomach gurgled. It would serve Ash right if I yacked all over him and the jeep.

I spun around. Behind us was a narrow path straight through to the desert and our disappearing tracks. Okay, that made absolutely no sense. How could I not see a giant ass hole in the wall? Oh, I know, because I refused to look. Who wants a front row seat for their death?

After tearing my gaze from the gap and appreciating the fact that I wasn't in the middle of a nightmare, I took in our surroundings. We sat in the middle of a canyon so narrow that I could reach out and touch both sides of the wall in some places. The towering sandstone seemed to go on forever, as did the slow-moving river winding through it. Like the rest of the desert, it was oddly beautiful and serene.

About fifty feet to our left stood a thicket of cypress and what looked to be olive trees, with six-foot-tall oleander bushes lining a winding path. Again, it was beautiful, but something felt...off. Like one of these things did not belong.

Which would probably be me.

"A little trust Gwendolyn." Ash's voice was soft, almost conciliatory.

I turned my death glare on him. I'd been so caught up in the oddly beautiful scenery I'd forgotten to be pissed off. But baby, I remembered now.

Ash frowned, as if unable to understand how my life flashing before my eyes would make me furious.

Whoever said violence was never the answer should be punched in the mouth. Rage warred with panic—and lost. Despite the Range Rover being topless, I couldn't breathe. It felt like someone had wrapped plastic wrap around my face.

My hands went to my throat as if a hunk of brisket rather than my freaking heart was lodged there.

A hand closed around my bicep, and I jerked my arm from his grip. Well, that was the plan, but Ash's strong fingers bit into my flesh.

I wasn't certain, but my head may have executed a three sixty. The only thing missing from my Exorcist reenactment was a priest, projectile vomit, and levitation.

"Let me go," I said, my voice echoing the rumbling thunder. "No. Gwendo—"

"I said let. Me. Go." My voice increased in volume with each word until I reached full on Banshee.

Clouds rolled in darkening the skies until it matched my mood. In other words, the once blue skies were gray, bleeding into black. Only this night sky held no shimmering stars or silvery moon. No, not only the sky, but the air around me had gathered an energy so filled with static that strands of Ash's hair rose, standing at attention.

The pounding in my ears increased its tempo until it became a roar of rage. Ash's lips moved, but I didn't hear, and I didn't give a damn. I filled my lungs with air. It was...different. Gone was the smell of the dry baked earth. It had been replaced by something sweeter, cleaner, almost like those minutes before a harsh summer rain.

Ozone.

Ash leaned closer, his lips moving, eyes filled with...not quite fear, but concern. Whether it was my ass or his he was worried about wasn't my damned problem, none of it was. My eyes narrowed, and I looked down at his hand then back into his bottomless eyes and bared my teeth.

A light show filled the darkened skies casting moving shadows along Ash's angular face. Followed by a rumbling thunder growing louder and seemingly closer as we sat staring at each other. My mother used to say that I shouldn't be afraid of thunderstorms because they were just angels bowling.

If that was the case, the echo of a strike bounced off the canyon walls.

"Listen I—" Ash yelled into the sudden swirling storm that matched the one roiling through my body.

"You what?" My words were punctuated with rage. That living breathing beast I'd kept tucked away, struggled to free itself, to lay waste to everything around me—including Ash.

Lightening hissed and cracked, followed by a vehicle rattling, retina singeing boom I felt down to my soul.

My skin was too hot, too tight, and too sensitive. Even the gentle breeze caressing my arms was unbearable. I panted, chest rumbling as I focused on breathing.

Inhale the joy that I still lived.

Exhale the incendiary fury. Ash was lucky. Had I controlled that lightning bolt he'd be as dead as I'd thought I was about to be.

Ash's touch gentled, and his thumb slid along my jaw. When had he moved his hands? "Gwendolyn..." This time his voice was more of a caress than a demand.

"If you say calm down," I said, my voice finally steady. "I swear you'll leave this place a eunuch."

"Ya kamar, I apologize." His hand stilled. "Slow your breathing. It's fine. I swear to you, never again will I do such a thing."

"I thought this was finally it." I inhaled, but it did nothing to unravel the knot in my chest. "I wasn't supposed to live this long."

Something flashed in his eyes. "Are you ill?"

I shook my head. The stress of the last twenty-four hours leaked from the corner of my eye, then rolled down the side of my nose. Damn it. I raised my hand to wipe it away, but Ash beat me to it.

"I'm an asshole." He blinked, studying me, watching me. Whether it was to see if I'd flip out a little more, I had no idea.

I frowned and would have pulled away from his touch had it not tethered me to reality. "If you're waiting for an argument—don't."

Ash swiped his thumb along my cheekbone. "I apologize," he said, sounding almost pained.

"Why do I get the feeling you don't use those words often?"

"Because that would be the truth." He cupped my neck, his long fingers curling along my nape. "Something else happened. What was that?"

Something the three of us—my insecurities, fears, and cynicism—would untangle later. Maybe there was a reason I hated monsters because the monster was me.

"It's okay," Ash whispered, his voice as soothing as a beer on a hot summer afternoon. He then kissed my forehead before blithely hopping out of the Range Rover. Before I realized what was happening, my door was opened, seatbelt undone, and I was in Ash's arms.

Finding a soft place to land against a hard body was good, but the shivers rattling my fillings—not so much.

Ash rubbed my back, whispering an unfamiliar language. It sounded Arabic but not. His tone made the hard vowels and crisp consonants solemn, sacred, and more than a little reverent.

The words made my bones ache. It was the lung-freezing fear that warned against the beast lurking in the darkness. A darkness that I'd stepped into willingly.

I tugged against Ash's hold, and he released me immediately, his gaze intense enough to set my locs on fire. "I brought lunch, but I'd understand..."

Was it shitty that his uncertainty brought me pleasure? Probably.

Did I feel an iota of guilt? Absolutely not.

I shook my head, exhaled a massive breath, then uncrossed my arms. "We're already here, and trust, I'm never coming back. So, I hope your stunt was worth it."

"I'm beginning to think that it was not. Am I forgiven?" he asked as he headed to the back of the Range Rover, withdrawing a blanket and a large covered rattan basket with long loopy handles.

"Not even close." I slid my jaw from side to side. Once again, I had a choice. I could stay good and truly pissed and make the day hell for both of us (which honestly, sounded like fun), or go with the flow and the suckage that I trusted Ash a little less. *Alex, I'll take making the best out of a bad situation for two thousand, please.* I finally shrugged, and didn't quite smile, but I wasn't frowning either. "But...depending on what's in the basket I might move you lower on the shit list."

"A woman who doesn't hold a grudge..." Ash nodded and turned around.

"Oh, I hold a grudge along with the best of them. Count yourself lucky. Now, show me your paradise." I scowled so hard I'd probably need Botox to fix it. "Just do me a favor, yeah?"

"Anything." He raised his right hand, and his face held so much solemnity, it gave me pause.

"No more painful surprises."

Chapter 9

As a lifelong student of tattooing and a holder of a M.F.A. in art history and painting, to say color was my life would be an understatement. The large pond ranging from the brightest cyan to areas as dark as a Georgia blueberry was so vibrant and overwhelming that I stood at its sandy edge with my fingers against my lips.

In other words, it was stunning.

The short walk from the Jeep had been tense, but once we passed through the trees, I forgot the hell I'd endured to get here. As far as I could tell, this place, this slice of heaven on terra firma hadn't seen a human in quite some time. Bright hued birds swooped and danced beneath the canopy of trees, periodically pausing in shafts of sunlight for duets or solos.

In other words, it was magical.

"Please tell me this isn't filled with piranhas or flesh-eating amoebas or something equally horrible and deadly," I called over my shoulder.

Ash paused from laying out our feast and sat cross-legged on the tan woolen blanket. "There is nothing that eats flesh in or out of the water in here. You're safe."

I squatted, swishing my fingers through the crystalline water, surprised at its warmth. With a quickness, I slipped off my boots and socks before gathering my djellaba and jerking it over my head. The word djellaba sounded so much cooler than muumuu or caftan. And this desert dwelling Mrs. Roper outfit had me feeling sexy.

Since Mr. Ash knew so much about me, I'm certain he was aware of most of my tattoos. I didn't try to hide them, for like scars, each piece told a story and meant something special. At least to me. But I'd placed my ink as to be able to display them when I chose.

My left arm was a full Asian themed sleeve that incorporated my lightning bolt, which was a birthmark, not an attack from an evil wizard. And my right arm was a half-sleeve, which I also designed, but it was more personal, an illustration of important moments and people in my life—including the night of the accident. The night my mother died.

The soft hiss let me know that Ash was very much paying attention. Was it my ass he was examining and appreciating, the crimson bikini, or the black and gray wings adorning my back?

Hello old friend insecurity.

I walked into the water until it covered my baby Buddha belly, pulled my shoulders back, raised my chin, then turned.

Dear ancestors.

My body temperature shot up fifteen degrees thanks to the blessedly shirtless Ash standing on the edge of the blanket. Unlike me, he'd worn cargo shorts under his djellaba, but that wasn't what held my attention. It was his chest.

Not the hard body, although that was better than nice, but his ink...

Despite not speaking Arabic, I've done enough tattoos in the language to recognize the hand of a master. But again, something was a little... off. Like his words earlier, it was almost Arabic, and all beautiful.

When I finally tore my gaze from the canvas of his chest, I raised my gaze to meet his. The heat in his eyes left my skin scorched and my body wanting.

That answered more than a few questions. One, I wasn't too old. Two, he liked ink, and most importantly, the scandalously small bikini I chose to wear. And three, he was absolutely going to get it.

And when I say it, I was talking about me.

Soft brushes against my thighs tore my gaze from Ash to the school of iridescent fish circling me. "This is so freaking cool." My voice was filled with awe, and that desire to make him die a slow and painful death for the ride of terror long gone.

All I wanted was to swim with Nemo's cousins.

"My view isn't too shabby either." He unbuttoned his shorts and pushed them to the ground.

And baby, I had a sudden urge to see the rest of the tattoo disappearing beneath the trunks. "Well, isn't this special, we match—again." I looked from his tight crimson swim shorts to my own bikini and chuckled.

"Yes, we do." He bit down on his lower lip, and his gaze slid down my body like a velvet touch.

"So, are you planning to join me or stare?"

"I've done enough of one, time for—"

Something solid and as hot as a rock spat from a volcano slammed against my back. Blazing agony shot through my torso, spreading outward as if that lightning from earlier had filled my body.

I gasped as my face hit the water, which wasn't the best of ideas since I hadn't grown gills in the last two seconds.

You know how they say your life flashes before your eyes when you die? Mine didn't. Everything moved in slow motion. Shimmering startled fish stared in judgement. Plants reached for me with long green arms beckoning me home, singing their siren's lullaby. Sleep. That sounded like a wonderful idea.

So, this was how it ended?

Well, at least when the reaper found me, I was having fun. Unlike my mother who'd been driving on a dark Texas highway. And wow, just my damned luck, I'll show up at the pearly gates in a freaking bikini.

The water faded from vivid blue to a dull gray as my vision narrowed into a pinpoint of pale light. Funny, I always believed that I'd fight death, go into the big bad beyond kicking and screaming. But why bother? This felt, so good, so right, so...

I sighed mentally, then surrendered to bliss.

Well, that's what it was supposed to be, but something fierce snatched me from the arms of slumber.

Oh crap.

I struggled, trying to free myself from the monster who had a hold of me, which sent skewering pain down my spine. If that wasn't bad enough, I coughed, and... ow, ow, ow.

Everything, even my hair hurt. Smashing into the wall would have been quicker—and less painful.

"Let me go," I said, or at least I thought I said.

My faceless enemy could have at least allowed a sister one last wicked act, like licking each one of Ash's tattoos. Some of them twice.

Ash hovered above me, my head now somehow on his lap. Again, he spoke that language, but this time it sounded like not one voice but many, surrounding us both with first discordance then harmony.

"C-cold," I whispered.

"You cannot leave." His strong hand scorched against my clammy cheek. Unfortunately, that was the only bit of me he warmed. It was like a lone match attempting to melt an iceberg.

"Y-you're not the boss of me." I coughed, (which I really needed to stop doing, because that shit hurt) and bits of blood blossomed on his forehead. Ew. "Wha-what happened?"

"Someone shot you. If you have believed nothing I've said, know that I will avenge you. But that vengeance will not be for your death. Do you hear me?"

Hallmark should make an I'll avenge you card with varying levels of mayhem, retribution, and bloodshed. I could totally see Ash's face on the front of one.

Storm clouds raced by, hiding the sun, and casting shifting shadows across Ash's face making him look less sexy hot guy and something a lot more sinister.

He leaned closer and gripped my chin. "Say yes."

The world, Ash, and everything else faded from an almost comforting gray to a fuzzy black and white like a television about to go on the fritz. I was so tired. Tired of fighting, tired of waiting, and so tired of being alone. Maybe on the other side of death I'd find my place. That place where I wasn't the freaky tattooed Black chick, or the nerd, or the only person in the family without real power. A place where I could simply be.

"Fucking say it." He shook me. "Say yes."

Ouch. That hurt, like for real. The chill that started at my extremities had now reached my core. My heartbeat thundered, the thick bass, pounding in my ears. The slower my heart beat, something else filled the spaces—whispers.

Soft feminine voices beckoned, caressing my soul like a compassionate breeze washing away the pain and filling me with...

Was that... happiness?

The chorus grew louder, more insistent. The voices separated, becoming solid. Bodies formed. The ancestors watched with eyes filled with both sadness and love. Faces from blackity black to brown and with even a couple of white folks sprinkled in the mix. From the center of the crowd walked the most welcome and familiar—Mom.

I dragged my gaze from my mother to the man who had no idea that he'd dodged a bullet. He stared at me, watching, waiting... but for what? Dude, I was dying here, and he had the nerve to be asking for shit?

Men.

What was that rattling sound?

"Gwendolyn Diane Carter, say yes," Ash whispered frantically.

Fine. If that is what it took for him to let me go in peace, and stop freaking shaking me, I'd tell him anything he wanted—even my weight. I licked my lips and whispered, "Yes."

But what I really meant was goodbye.

Chapter 10

I'd left paradise and entered a funky acid trip. Colors swirled around me, from yellow to orange to green to purple and back again. Of course, my death spiral would be as weird as the living portion of the program.

My soul's psychedelics slowed before fading, settling on a pale orange tinged with pink that reminded me of a tropical sunrise. Before I could settle in and enjoy the view, my E-ticket ride came to a screeching, bone rattling halt. Wait, if I was dead, which I'm pretty sure I was, did I have bones?

I didn't get to fully examine myself, or answer the question, because...where was I? No pearly gates, no lake of fire, no colorless limbo.

How had I landed on an iridescent beach?

Odd, but an improvement over the whole burning in hell bit.

I twisted my back left, then right. No pain, no twinges of discomfort. Then, I placed my hand over my chest, and ... Holy crap, I was like a whole two sizes smaller.

Oh yeah. I had definitely gone to the good place.

"Why wouldn't you?" a warm voice said from behind me.

I spun around and stared. "Mom?" There she was, wearing a simple mauve shift with the matching polish on her toes disappearing into the sparkling sands as she moved closer.

"Hey sweetheart, I'm glad it took this long to see you again."

Pressure pulsated against my eyes, and my nose tingled, the warning signs of an impending ugly snot-filled cry. "Is this—" What if this was just a dream? If so, I didn't want to wake up, and I sure as heck didn't want to waste time bawling.

She closed the distance between us, sliding her hands down my arms and interlacing her fingers with mine, holding tight as if afraid to lose me again. "Baby, I am so proud of you. I hope your life was *everything* you wanted it to be."

We always used to joke how different we were. I was all about bright and bold primary colors, but she was muted and soft. She was nineteen fifties housewife while I was Black pinup and rockabilly.

There was so much I wanted to ask, so much to say, but the first complete sentence to roll past my lips was, "You look so pretty." I inwardly cringed. What a dork.

Her face brightened even more, and her luscious alto laughter, always sweet, was a musical balm to my heart. "Oh, there are so many people I want you to meet. I have a zillion questions about the family and your life. But we can do that later. There's plenty of time."

"Like an eternity?"

She nodded, and for the first time since I'd arrived, my mother looked sad.

"It's okay, Mom. I mean, at least I have company, right?"

Mom slipped her arm through mine and led me across the sands. "You always said your heaven was a tropical beach."

"How do you know that?"

"Because I watched when possible. You're my baby, how could I not?"

"But I talked to you, erected altars, placed your favorite foods on them, and showed up every day. Why didn't you answer?" I stopped moving.

"Because I couldn't—none of us could. There is so much I should have shared, but I wanted you to hold on to your precious innocence. When I decided it was time..." Her fingers flittered to the strand of perfect white pearls lying at the base of her throat. "Well, it was too late. But we played the song in the bar, and the smoke alarm was a nice touch." She watched me, hope blooming across her face, the same rich brown as my own. "At least, I thought so."

"Thanks, but you know me, I found a way to screw it up." I nodded, interlaced our fingers, and smiled. As far as days went, this one had been a doozy. What I needed was a freaking bar and a bottle of bourbon.

"All you have to do is will it so." Mom started walking again, pulling me with her.

"Did I say that out loud?"

"No, words aren't necessary. Not here. Look." She pointed down the beach. "They're all waiting for you."

"Who?"

"Your ancestors."

The closer we got, the more I could see the men and women and even a few children, smiling, waiting, and waving. If love had a physical manifestation, the threads of warmth pouring from those who came before me intertwined with my mother's love to give me the warmest of hugs. Their affection was like a soft fuzzy blanket, or that oversized cashmere sweater on a frigid winter day.

This, this was what I'd been missing and what I'd spend the rest of—

My birthmark tingled, but I ignored it, fascinated by the smiling waiting people. "I'd really like to meet my great-grandmother. Is she here?"

Mom hesitated, exhaled, then squeezed my hand. "No, but there's a way for you to speak with her. It's going to take a minute."

"Why?"

"Let's just say our family tree is... I don't even know where to begin."

"Mom, I was raised by a vampire. Just start at the beginning."

"If I had..." She jerked me to a stop and stepped in front of me like a mama bear protecting her cub.

"What's wrong?" My birthmark went from tingling to four-alarm. "Ouch." Since I hadn't received the Hoodoo Heaven handbook, I tried to think away the pain. Hey, if it worked for bourbon, it couldn't hurt to try.

Or maybe not.

I stared at my tattoo covered arm. There, amongst the Japanese themed motif, with its lotus blossoms, abstract koi fish, and the obligatory dragon was the small odd-looking mark that always reminded me of a violent storm. Except today, it twirled and shifted as streaks of light traveled down my wrist, across the bones in the back of my hand to my fingers.

Streams of electricity, three brilliant white streaks shot from my fingers hit the water, then skipped across it like flat stones. I gaped, then turned to Mom. This was absolutely one of those things that needed explaining. Like immediately.

This whole Thor moment was freaking me the heck out. But it wasn't the lightning bolts shooting from my left hand that had my mother shook. No, she stared at the fiery fingers blossoming on my right arm like a mirage.

Whoa. That was awesome.

Maybe I was getting called up to meet the big guy, or woman, or whatever. If that was the case, I had a whole list of suggestions to make Earth a little less...well—hellish.

"What have you done?" The terror in my mother's wide eyes was something I'd never thought to see again. It was like the night of the accident, tears glistening like diamonds on her lower lids before she took her last breath.

When I reached out to touch her face, Mom backed away, shaking her head. "Not again, no, not again..."

"Mommy, what's wrong?"

Instead of answering, she slapped her hand over her mouth, which did nothing to silence the guttural moan rising from the deepest darkest part of her soul.

"It's okay. Look." I extended my arm. "It hurts a whole lot less than old sparky." I wiggled the fingers of what will now and forever be dubbed my Thor hand. Luckily the external light show was over. But under my skin, sparks like fireflies traveled up my arm. Which was freaky, but cool.

Someone cleared their throat. Someone who was obviously not my mother, since Mom was full-on keening now. Which, by the way, was more unnerving than anything else that had happened today. This was the moment. The one in all the movies when the hero, believing they'd escaped, lowered their guard and got creamed.

But come on, I'd already battled death and won, how much... I shook my head. Nope, no way was I going to ask that question, not even silently. What you think about you bring about and all that shit. What I also wasn't going to do was look at the new guest.

"What you're looking at Gwendolyn is guilt," said a familiar, lightly accented and dangerous baritone. The voice I'd often compared to a purr had become a lethal growl.

I spun around and gaped as I shook my head. What was happening? Did they like serve 'shrooms in heaven? Because I must be high. Then reality hit me so hard I staggered. I wasn't sure if it was nausea or panic clawing at my throat, but I panted, struggling to breath.

Noooo. Not only did my carelessness kill me, but... If this was heaven, there was only one answer to why Ash was here.

I rubbed my knuckles against my chest and retreated, moving away from both him and my mother. "I'm so sorry," I whispered.

Ash smiled, and once again in this perfect place, with this perfect man, I was Eve, and before me stood my sexy shining apple.

"I killed you." That happiness I'd felt seconds ago with Mom, was long gone, replaced by a guilt so heavy I had no idea how to get from under it. He must hate me. That vengeance Ash spoke about wielding like an ancient warlord, was about to land on me like a shit-ton of pissed off bricks.

I sucked in a breath, then exhaled before facing my fate. Finally, I asked, "Ash, what are you doing here?"

He watched me for what felt like hours. The weight of his gaze, like so much of him felt immense, the moment important. I really would have liked to have spent more time with him on Earth. The man was an odd combination of hot, scary, funny, and almost intimidating.

And I liked him—which led him to his doom. Sorry wasn't a big enough word to encompass my emotions, I prayed that Ash could read the sorrow etched on my soul. After living almost forty-five years, I'd finally met the one. A man who could handle my bullshit. A man who needed nothing from me, not fame, not money, not notoriety.

A man who would have been easy to love.

Finally, his face softened. The smile he gifted me was so soft, so precious, that I knew that regardless of what happened on the beach, I'd treasure it always. Ash extended a hand as he walked past my mother, standing close enough that the subtle scent of his cologne enveloped me. "Come Gwendolyn, you said yes." When I placed my fingers in his, Ash squeezed my hand and lowered his voice. "You now belong to me."

The End... for now

Ramblings of a messy mind

I don't know about you, but I'm tired of being erased in popular media. Seriously, as women, if we don't fit in a specific tiny box—too bad, so sad. So, rather than complain, I began writing the book I wanted to read. I only had a few requirements. It needed to be:

1. fun

2. inclusive

3. include magic and murder

4. have a bunch of hot guys (for me)

5. feature and celebrate women over forty kicking ass, taking names, and if they wanted... getting a partner along the way.

In Elizabeth Gilbert's book, Big Magic, she talks about ideas floating out in the ether tempting us to grab hold of and create something magnificent. A group of authors-the Fab 13-had the same idea. (if you haven't read any of their books, what are you waiting for?)

My series Boudin, Barbecue, and Hoodoo is a love letter of sorts to women of all ages, including myself. We are never too old or too young to embrace our magic. As the eternal optimist, I believe we're all more alike than different. As humans, we want to be seen, understood, loved, and respected.

I may not get everything right, but damn it, I'm going to keep trying. If you're reading this, I both see and appreciate you.

Also by Reggi Dupree

Return to Hoodoo

Return to Hoodoo

Welcome to Hoodoo, Texas—Mayberry with magic, midlife, and a dash of murder.

I expected my forties to be filled with imbalanced hormones and an ex-husband or two. Instead, I died for the second time, was gifted a Thor hand, then a summons to my hometown of Hoodoo, Texas.

The one place I swore never to return after being accused of murder.

Now the plan was to get in, accept the mysterious inheritance, then get the heck out of Dodge. The good part was that the windfall came with a lot of zeros. Unfortunately, it was also accompanied by a dilapidated haunted mansion and one heck of a stipulation.

If I refused the money or Azure House, the fortune will go to a stranger.

Now, I'm stuck wrangling unruly relatives, ghostly servants, grumpy vampires, and a vindictive ex who happens to be a werewolf as well as the sheriff. Add a sexy and perhaps not quite human mogul and you have the recipe for disaster.

And if that's not bad enough, witches are dropping dead in Hoodoo. Guess who's at the top of the suspect list?

Return to Hoodoo is a paranormal women's fiction novel set in a world best described as True Blood meets Queen Sugar.

About the Author

There's something about magic, action, and the supernatural that calls to my wicked soul. I enjoy most genre fiction, but am drawn to heroines like me and my weird circle of friends: not so slim, not that young, and even a wee bit cranky. But we also find joy and laughter, even in the darkest of times.

I fill my books with adventure, magic, loss, love, and casts bursting with diversity. Seriously, how boring would life be if we were all the same?

Okay, now the personal stuff.

I married the first boyfriend who made it past the four-month mark. Since we've been hitched over thirty-five years, I'm thinking he just might stick. The cat? Well, he's too spoiled and way too stubborn to move off the couch.